Uncaged

I0666918

No Rival #7

Charity Parkerson

--Warning: This book is intended for

readers over the age of 18.

ISBN-10:1-946099-10-4

ISBN-13:978-1-946099-10-5

Introduction

Most people's soulmates bring light, joy, and happiness into their lives. Jozsua's brought death.

As the younger brother of a notorious crime lord, Jozsua's life has been anything but normal. Mostly, it's been spent hiding out in the open. He's been fighting on the MMA circuit while trying to keep his sister-in-law and niece safe from the remnants of his brother's reputation since his death. The only break Jozsua has ever had from the monotony of life on the run was that one time he fell in love with a killer.

Dmitry's been called a lot of things—murderer, psychopath... hitman. Seeing how it's all true, he doesn't let it get to him. Since he's a sociopath, it wouldn't bother him, even if it could. When he's sent to infiltrate the Danshov family, he also doesn't let the fact that he'll have to kill them all one day stop him from pursuing Jozsua. After all, he's not one to deny himself when someone catches his eye. However, once Jozsua is in his bed and in his head, Dmitry can't shake him.

Now, with the job he was hired to complete out of the way, Dmitry has his sights set on Jozsua once again. With all his secrets on the table, he has one last job to do—to win back the man who gave him a conscience. The man whose brother Dmitry killed.

Author note: This is a dark story not meant for all readers. Jozsua and Dmitry's love is borderline insanity, but it's their love story.

Prologue

Two years earlier...

"Konstantin Danshov was found dead overnight..."

Those words continued to play in Josh's head over and over again as he ate up the floor of his living room. He'd practically dug a ditch with his pacing as he tried repeatedly to get hold of Dmitry. Each time, the phone rang with no end in sight. Not even a voicemail box magically appeared to save his sanity.

Konstantin had been more like a father than an older brother. Both sons of a Russian mafia leader, their futures had been set at birth. Shortly before Jozsua turned thirteen, their father had been found shot to death in his office. Konstantin had brought Jozsua to live with him in the States, changing his name to Josh and hoping the Danshov family would forget he existed. His brother had wanted nothing more than for Josh to have a normal life, as much as anyone could with mafia ties and a brother who played professional hockey. It had been too late for Konstantin. As the oldest son of Boris Danshov, he'd been sent to the US, using his goaltending talent as cover to set up family operations. He was in too deep. Still, he'd managed—for the most part—to keep Josh out of things. Of course, Josh had still spent thirteen years with their father. He'd been taught to fight. Done and seen things he couldn't take back. Lost a sense of normalcy and right and wrong. Even living with Kon hadn't been perfect. He'd been exposed to things regular people were not... and fallen in love with a killer.

Josh tried Dmitry's phone again, praying he'd pick up. When Dmitry's thick Russian accent rang through the line, Josh's knees almost gave out.

"Hello?"

Josh didn't waste words. "Was it you? Did you do it? Did you kill my brother?" His voice cracked on the final word, but he had to know. For a full minute, silence met his question. He felt every second in his soul. Each one that ticked by damned Dmitry a little more.

"Yes."

A roar of denial ripped from Josh's throat as he hurled the phone away from him. The hole it left in the wall upon impact wasn't enough. He searched the room with his gaze, looking for an outlet. He wanted to tear everything down. The whole goddamn world. Snatching up the lamp, he yanked the cord from the wall before heading for the TV. The lamp's wooden base made the perfect bat as he smashed the screen. Nothing was spared in his fury. By the time the storm passed, his coffee table scattered the room in splinters and blood dripped from Josh's knuckles. His chest heaved from the exertion and sweat ran down his spine.

None of it mattered. His brother had loved him. Trusted him above all others. Given Josh the freedom he himself had lost. In the end, Josh had been the one who'd killed him by falling in love with the enemy.

Chapter 1

"We've been thinking."

Josh glanced up from his task of replacing the weights he'd been using. Max and Ryan were hovering.

"I'm waiting," Josh said, urging Ryan on. They'd met briefly on a few occasions. Not to mention, Max owned the fitness center they were currently standing in, Grid Iron. Still, Josh could think of only a few times when they'd seen one another, and even fewer when they'd spoken.

"We've been thinking," Ryan repeated. "You should join us at Affinity some night."

Since he'd run into the pair at a local dance hall while having drinks with his sister-in-law, they'd purposely stepped into Josh's path more than he liked. It wasn't that they didn't seem like decent men. For Josh, it was more that he was not a decent guy. They needed to steer clear.

"What is this Affinity?" Josh heard the question leave his lips as if coming from another. He hated talking to anyone. At home, he was free to be himself. Kip and Cameron knew most of his secrets. In fact, they had a few of their own. In public, Josh had to be someone else. He had to concentrate on his every word. Even after years of living in the States, his Russian accent was thick. He tried to keep it hidden without much luck. Instead, he usually didn't speak at all.

Ryan and Max exchanged glances. Josh bit back a sigh. It didn't seem they would be getting to the point anytime soon. Setting his hands on his hips, he waited. As far as Josh had observed, Ryan seemed to be the outgoing one while Max was more intense. He could picture them together. Josh ground his back teeth against the image. No doubt they were beautiful. Love was gorgeous sometimes. Not for him.

"The thing is," Ryan said.

"We've been thinking," Max said at the same time.

Josh sighed. "Back to this, are we?"

The pair smiled. An unwanted wave of desire crashed over Josh. He kept his features blank by sheer will. They were a sexy couple. No doubt, people everywhere fantasized about a night between them. But Josh didn't mess with men. Not anymore. Not since... He turned away and grabbed the abandoned weights, hoping they wouldn't see the longing—the way he craved handing over the control.

"I've got shit to do today," Josh said.

Even he heard the way his voice had thickened. He cleared his throat. "This Affinity sounds like a club, correct?" He hoped the men would accept his olive branch. It wasn't their fault he was the way he was.

The men nodded. Ryan's smile brightened. Max smoldered. The hair stood on the back of Josh's neck.

"It's an exclusive one," Ryan offered.

"One where we're members," Max added.

Ryan nodded. "You should come with us."

The man's invitation sounded the same as the devil luring someone into signing documents. The uneasy feeling in Josh's gut intensified.

"And you're extending this invitation to me, because..."

Both men smiled, but Ryan answered. "We love Kip and would like to know you better as well."

His discomfort fled. Josh snorted. "No. You wouldn't. Thanks for the offer, but I think I'll pass."

"Are you sure?" Ryan sounded ready to let it drop.

Max spoke up. "Aren't you tired of hiding?"

Josh's fingers went cold as he dropped the final weights back into place. There was something in Max's tone, as if he knew. When Josh didn't respond, Max took a step closer. A plain black card appeared beneath Josh's nose. A single word "Affinity" stared up at him. Josh didn't take it.

"If you don't want to go with us, you

should still go. No good can come of pretending to be someone you're not. Trust me. I know."

Without thought, Josh's fingers clasped the card. He flipped it over, inspecting the back. It felt heavier than he expected—as if it was a passkey rather than a business card. Other than the name, the card was blank.

"Seems a bit of a useless thing since there's no information on it."

Max's eyes flashed with something Josh didn't understand. "Say you'll go. If not with us, then I'll give you the address." Max was hypnotizing Josh with his stare. Josh couldn't look away from his amber gaze. "Either way, show the card at the door for entry."

"This club is sounding very secret-like." Josh didn't bother trying to tone down his accent. It was as if Max weaved a spell around him. The man's mouth lifted in one corner. Against his will, Josh's gaze dropped to Max's gorgeous lips.

"Of course it is," Max said, still smirking. "Most fetish clubs are."

If there was a competition for keeping a straight face, Josh felt he earned the gold. He was shocked, but then again, he wasn't. There was something inherently sexual about Max. Some people were charming. Others were outgoing. Max was temptation. He made people burn whether he intended it to happen or not. The man couldn't choose to not be a hard-on waiting to happen. It was built in—an intricate part of his being. Ryan was the flirt and—no doubt—up for anything. But Max, he was a different flavor—like an LSD-laced lollipop. One lick was all it took to enslave a man. Just like the drug, that wasn't a good thing. Then again, all Josh's favorite things were deadly.

"What time and where?"

The matching smiles meeting his question had Josh's mouth going dry. Perhaps it had been a long time since he'd been with a man, but he wasn't opposed to having two. Now was as good a time as any to set a match to what was left of his life.

* * *

If not for the lone man standing in the shadows and occasionally ushering people inside the nondescript door, Josh would've thought the address Ryan had given him was a joke. Affinity was right there, in the middle of everything and underneath some of the poshest stores in Vegas. The shops had long since closed for the night. It still seemed odd for such tawdry happenings to be going on right beneath where people got their Botox done during the day.

Headlights momentarily blinded Josh as a truck pulled into the parking lot. It seemed to Josh he should at least be a little nervous. As usual, he felt nothing. He'd died the day his brother had. His heart continued to beat against all laws of nature. As he watched Ryan and Max climb from their truck, Josh realized they could've shown up or not. Neither outcome would've fazed him. It had been this way since... Josh ruthlessly cut off his thoughts before they took hold and watched as Ryan and Max headed for the door.

He wouldn't think tonight. Instead, he concentrated on taking in the vision of Ryan and Max. They were gorgeous. Ryan's green eyes always sparkled with devilry. They would be amazing. Tonight wasn't about that either. There'd been this invisible line in the sand he'd created in his mind he'd been refusing to cross. Max was right. Josh was hiding his true nature, but not for any of the reasons they would suspect. No. Josh had known if he touched another man, he'd permanently lose someone he'd already lost. Tonight, he was killing something already long dead to everyone except him.

Dmitry.

The name floated across Josh's mind. He ruthlessly tore his thoughts away. Josh waited until after he watched the men go inside the private club before stepping from his truck. Josh's skin crawled, as if invisible eyes followed his every move. He fought the urge to glance over his shoulder. By the time Josh reached the doorman, his shoulders were nearly cramping beneath the strain.

The man working the entrance seemed every bit as nondescript as the door he guarded until he met Josh's stare. His golden gaze reminded Josh so much of a lion's, he had to stop himself from saying as much. Instead, he passed the card over. "I'm meeting someone."

The man's mouth quirked. "Isn't everyone?" Holy Hell. His voice. Wow. Josh swallowed back a hum. If the dude's day job wasn't phone sex, it was a damn shame. "What's your name?"

"What's yours?" Josh asked before he could stop it. The man was fucking Josh's ears. He had to know.

A low rumble of laughter slipped from the man's lips and caressed Josh's skin. He flashed an electronic tablet Josh's way. "It's for the reservation."

"It's for me," Josh shot back.

The man's lips twisted as he visibly fought not to smile. "I'm Isaac."

"Josh Salko."

"Intriguing." Isaac said, apropos of nothing, but fascinating Josh nonetheless. Isaac swiped his finger across the device. "Nice. You have a private room and special instructions. I'll show you the way." Josh had no problem falling into step behind Isaac. He scanned a keycard across the keypad, unlocking the door. Josh's gaze slid down the man's body, taking in his chocolate skin and runner's build. The ass was nice too. Josh shook his head. It was as if Max and Ryan's proposition had unleashed something inside him. Josh still wasn't sure how he felt about it. As he entered the building, Josh realized he'd soon find out.

The door led to a darkened hallway followed by a sharp turn and a set of stairs, leading down into the unknown. With Isaac leading the way, Josh allowed the man to steer him toward whatever plans Ryan and Max had in mind. Sultry music and low moans met them halfway down the stairs. The temperature dropped the farther they descended. The first wisp of sheer lace came into view. Josh held his breath, expecting anything. See-through curtains hung from the ceiling to the floor. They danced in time with the air blowing from the vents, giving everything a surreal edge. The thin scraps of material did nothing to hide the erotic scenes taking place on the other side.

Josh's steps slowed as he caught sight of a man on his knees, head bowed and hands bound. His nude body and submissive pose gave the illusion of helplessness.

Josh knew from experience that wasn't the case. Handing over control took more power than it gave. Josh didn't realize he'd stopped moving until Isaac motioned him forward.

"Your room is this way."

The softly spoken announcement had Josh snapping to attention. The longer he walked, the more private the rooms became. Sheer curtains became velvet. Velvet turned to actual walls and doors. The third door they reached, Isaac opened, waving Josh in ahead of him. It was empty—with the exception of chains hanging from the ceiling.

"Strip," Isaac said as he pulled the door closed behind them.

Josh's eyebrows tried hitting his hairline at the demand.

Isaac's gaze swept down Josh's body.

"Unless you're shy."

At the challenging note in Isaac's voice, Josh pulled his shirt over his head and tossed it aside. Satisfaction roared through him at the way Isaac's eyes flashed with hunger. "Your host will be with you shortly and it's obvious they think you're a runner. I've been instructed to make sure you're chained and blindfolded." Josh thought they probably had a good point. He might bolt. Isaac met and held his stare. "For the record, this is the most tempted I've ever been to put in a request to join."

This man was a sexual deviant. Josh felt it in his bones.

"Maybe you should keep your pants on after all," Isaac added.

Josh nodded, incapable of speaking. If he lost his pants, he might just ask Isaac to stay. The closer he came to feeling a man's touch again, the stronger his cravings became. He missed the hard muscles. The rough touch. The devastation.

Isaac motioned Josh toward the chains. "Do you have a problem with being bound? Everything we do here must be agreed upon upfront."

Josh eyed the metal shackles. He lifted his arms in the air toward them. "I'm fine with this." The words slipped past his lips even as his mind drifted away.

Cold steel kept his hands bound to the headboard. Josh didn't know how he hadn't ripped the wooden piece down. He'd been straining hard against the oak rungs from what felt like hours as Dmitry spread his ass cheeks wide and massaged his prostate. It wasn't enough to get him off, and Dmitry fucking knew it. This man had a gift when it came to keeping Josh hanging on the edge.

Oil coated his cock, balls, and asshole, easing the way for the selection of toys Dmitry had chosen for the night. The sweat coating his skin made it hard to tell the difference between it and the lubricant. Dmitry stroked Josh's oblique, barely brushing Josh's erection with the side of his hand. His dick twitched as if trying to get closer.

"You are so beautiful, Jozsua."

Josh took in the picture Dmitry presented. His shirt hung open, exposing a gorgeous chest. Dmitry was perfect in Josh's eyes. Only the way his shirt clung to his overheated skin and the huskiness in Dmitry's voice gave any hint as to how turned on the man was. Dmitry was the master at hiding his emotions. The way he always kept his every thought hidden made Josh want to make the man work *twice as hard to keep him. Because, for Josh, it was love. It was love so fucking deep and wide there was no chance he wouldn't drown. Possibly Dmitry might never love him in return, but he'd damn well remember Josh until the day he died.*

"Don't look so intense. I'll be back in an hour to set you free."

Josh blinked at the man standing before him. He'd gotten lost. The arms stretched above his head were the same ones that had been handcuffed to the bed so long ago. They didn't feel the same. Now, they just felt cold. Isaac pulled a blindfold from his back pocket and slipped it over Josh's head, plunging him into darkness.

"So tempted," Isaac said, doing a good job of pulling Josh from his bleak memories.

"Me too," Josh admitted before the man could slip away. Isaac's sexy low chuckle followed him to the door. The blindfold heightened his senses. He listened to Isaac's retreating footsteps and his near silent exit. Once alone, Josh inhaled a slow breath through his nose and tried pushing everything from his mind. An image of Ryan and Max filled his head. Both men had gorgeous bodies, as any fitness club owner and defense teacher would. Ryan matched Josh in height while Max stood a few inches shy of six feet. They were gorgeous. He'd once accidentally walked in on them kissing inside one of the fitness club's many classrooms. Josh tried backing quietly away. Ryan's gaze had locked on to him before he could escape. Perhaps that had been the moment he'd given himself away to the pair. His body's reaction to the heated scene had been swift. Fire had raced through him. In that moment, he'd missed the erections bumping. The animalistic kisses. The beard burn.

The muscles in Josh's stomach clenched. He hadn't let another man touch him since Dmitry. It was his way of punishing himself. At least, that was what he told himself. He should be punished. No penance would ever be enough.

*

The guy working the door of Affinity had been easy to bribe. Dmitry watched as he escorted Jozsua inside. With his phone balanced on one knee, he ran through everything about the man's body that had changed. His hair was still some crazy shade of blue, but it looked darker. He was harder, with more muscles, but then again, Jozsua had always been more amazing than most.

A thick layer of sweat coated Jozsua's skin, making Dmitry wonder if he'd slip the cuffs keeping him chained to the bed. When they'd started this game, the room had been freezing. Now, even with his shirt unbuttoned and hanging open, the two halves clung to his overheated skin. Jozsua had more stamina and self-control than anyone Dmitry had ever encountered. The blue-haired punk. Fuck. The way he watched Dmitry's every move, waiting for more of whatever sexual torture Dmitry had to offer, was intoxicating. Sometimes, he couldn't help but wonder what would happen if he hurt Jozsua. Not enough to damage him or mar his beautiful skin. Just enough to break his focus.

Dmitry peeled off his clothes before setting one knee on the foot of the bed. He held Jozsua's gaze as the other knee joined the first. As he crawled up Jozsua's body, a *dark hunger rose inside him. Electricity filled the air between them. He'd worked his ass off to lure this man into his bed. Jozsua had made Dmitry work twice as hard to keep him there. Dmitry had never wanted anyone more. When he reached Jozsua's midsection, something inside Dmitry gave way. His inner demons demanded satisfaction. Without thought, he dipped his head and bit Jozsua's hip— hard.*

The guttural moan coming from the back of Jozsua's throat was his undoing. No more teasing or torture. Dmitry's lips brushed Jozsua's crown. This wasn't something he did. People serviced him, not the other way around. The way Jozsua writhed beneath him was too much. He needed Jozsua to come undone. The man's cock slid across Dmitry's tongue before he accepted it would happen. Male salt coated

31

his taste buds as pre-cum escaped Jozsua. Like crack, its flavor was an instant addiction. Maybe he was hooked on the taste of a turned on male. Dmitry knew the truth. It was Jozsua. He owned Dmitry.

Saliva dripped from Dmitry's chin. Jozsua's dick sawed in and out of Dmitry's mouth. At some point, it had become a mindless act. His brain had been busy working through his emotions. Dmitry's name slipped past Jozsua's lips, sounding like a prayer. A tidal wave of emotions overcame him. Every secret he kept became crystal clear alongside the lies he'd told himself since setting eyes on Jozsua. Cum filled his mouth. Dmitry swallowed without thought. Juices dripped from his lips onto Jozsua's stomach as he surged upward, claiming Jozsua's mouth. There was no protest, only a struggle to get closer.

All thoughts of calculating each move

fell away. Without a thought for protection and with nothing more than the oils they'd been toying with to ease his path, Dmitry pushed his way inside Jozsua's ass. The sounds coming from Jozsua's throat vibrated around their entwined tongues, driving Dmitry's lust. Tight heat squeezed his dick, dragging moans from Dmitry. He tore his mouth away, needing to taste Jozsua's sweat. His teeth scraped Jozsua's jaw, taking in the rough bristles there. Jozsua strained against his restraints, begging Dmitry to fuck him harder. They were a dynamite C-4 crockpot bomb ready to level an entire block. What they had was fucking beautiful.

"I love you," Dmitry said, hearing the first-time confession as loud as gunfire and not caring. It was true. He needed Jozsua to know.

"Oh, God, Dmitry. I love you too." The

deep chorus of Jozsua's words rang true and sang to Dmitry's heart, feeding the dark sickness growing inside him.

As his balls tightened, anticipating release, another emotion grew as well. Rage. The idea of anyone harming what belonged to him had Dmitry craving the sight of their life leaving their eyes. His orgasm hit, bowing his back and sending waves of ecstasy rolling through him. Dmitry sucked Jozsua's skin, attempting to soothe the beast inside. Nothing worked. The growled words tore from his throat, sounding demonic mixed with their ragged breaths.

"Streets will run red before I let anyone touch you."

It was still true. The face of his phone lit, pulling him away from his memories, and letting him know the deed was done. Jozsua needed to remember who he belonged to. He feared, if it didn't happen soon, the streets of Vegas would run red. After all, he couldn't have his man accepting propositions as he had tonight. The next one might be real. So too would be the bloodshed.

*

The door opened. A cold blast of air washed over Josh's bare chest. One set of footsteps crossed the room. They were soft—like a wraith. He tried to decide which of the men walked in such a way. Neither Ryan nor Max came to mind. The cologne hit Josh first—leather and spice. Oxygen became harder to come by. His breath quickened. That scent. It tickled the back of his mind. The footsteps stopped before reaching him.

Fingertips brushed his stomach. Fire flared in their path. The button loosened on his jeans. His zipper slid down. Each touch was light and PG13. Josh's blood boiled like he was ass up, getting fucked—hard. It had been so goddamn long since he'd felt anything at all. Cool air brushed his erection. Still no contact came with his cock. Josh bit the inside of his cheek hard enough to taste blood. He'd missed the raging desire. This crazy feeling of losing control had eluded him for way too long. His captor moved closer. The heat from the other man's skin engulfed Josh.

"Jozsua."

Josh's heart skipped a beat as the softly spoken word brushed across his ear. The sudden onslaught of heart palpitations had nothing to do with lust. Only two men in the world had ever called him by that name. One was dead. The other...

"Dmitry." The man's name slipped past Josh's lips, sounding like a benediction. He forgot his surroundings. Time slipped away. His knees weakened. If his hands hadn't been chained above his head, Josh would've hit the floor. The scent of spicy cologne filled his nostrils and memories crowded his brain. Phantom sweat and male salt coated his taste buds as the image of the last night they spent together filled his mind. Even though the crippling pain was slow to set in, the power of his loss was no less overwhelming. So many things. This man, he'd stolen so much from Josh.

His brain screamed and fought against his body. He didn't want to burn for Dmitry. Dmitry's fingertips seared Josh's skin with every brush as he trailed his fingers down Josh's torso. As always with Dmitry, Josh was more aware of the man's every touch than anything else in his life. With his shoulder, he pushed the blindfold up, needing the man to see his hatred. Max and Ryan were nowhere to be seen.

He hadn't imagined only one set of foot-falls. Their gazes met. The blue eyes that were so light in coloration they were al-most gray were the first thing he'd fallen hard for when he'd met Dmitry. They stared back at him now. Josh squeezed his eyes shut against the sight, wishing he'd left the blindfold in place. There was love and then there was the sickness he'd always felt for Dmitry.

Dmitry's fingers brushed Josh's hip as he pushed Josh's jeans lower.

"Please?"

At Josh's plea, Dmitry moved even closer. Josh turned his head, pressing his face to his arm to stop the man's lips from touching his. Instead of forcing him, Dmitry brushed a light kiss across the shell of Josh's ear. His lips moved lower before he opened his mouth over the cords of Josh's neck. Hyperventilation looked like a real possibility. He couldn't let this man touch him. There was no way to stop it. Why was he here? How had this nightmare taken life?

Dmitry stroked Josh's hip again. "Please don't do this," Josh begged, beyond caring how despondent he sounded. He was desperate. This would break him. Staying away from Dmitry was the only way he'd held tight to his sanity these past couple of years.

Proving there was no mercy in Dmitry's heart, his fingers encircled Josh's erection. That part of his body knew what Dmitry could do and refused to obey Josh's mind. He'd never been more torn between desire and hatred.

"I'm sorry," Dmitry whispered, taking away the last of Josh's hope. "I can't stop. You shouldn't hate yourself for this. It's out of your control. Since you cannot hate me more," Dmitry said, as he slipped to his knees, taking Josh's jeans with him as he went. Josh's eyes betrayed him. His chin hit his chest so he could stare down at Dmitry as the man took him between his lips. Dmitry was wrong. Hatred had no basement. It was a bottomless pit—one Josh couldn't stop falling into. Neither could he ask Dmitry to stop.

As the man's tongue curled around Josh's dick, tears pressed at the backs of his eyes. They weren't in helpless frustration as they should've been. They were for his loss. His broken heart. All he'd been left with when this man had destroyed everything. The dark blond hair covering Dmitry's head and chin were as familiar as looking into a mirror for Josh. He'd ripped himself into pieces so many times trying to make this man whole.

Tilting his chin up, Josh stared at his

hands, hoping if he didn't see Dmitry, then he could force the pleasure to dissipate. Maybe then he could think. Even the loss of Dmitry's gorgeous face didn't deter Josh's mind. It already knew the man he loved more than life was on his knees. He felt every taste bud. Josh's erection slipped from Dmitry's mouth. Josh bit back a cry of denial.

"Tell me to stop," Dmitry demanded.

He couldn't. Josh's throat wouldn't work. He feared it might never work again.

*

Jesus. He'd known it would be bad. Dmitry thought he'd mentally prepared himself for this encounter. He'd lost count of the number of lectures he'd given himself. There'd been no need to harden his heart. Dmitry didn't have one. What little humanity he'd once had belonged to

Jozsua. Not a single explanation came to mind for the tightness in his chest. He'd watched tears fill Jozsua's eyes before the man had tilted his head back and focused on the ceiling. There was no denying matters. He'd done this to Jozsua. Never in a million years would Dmitry have believed himself capable of bringing Jozsua so low. In this case, he was hurting Jozsua so he could fix him—like re-breaking a bone to set it properly.

Jozsua's cock slid across Dmitry's tongue, making his eyes fall closed. His taste buds were in flavor heaven. As much as Dmitry knew there was no expiration date on grief, he couldn't give Jozsua more time. His patience had a limit. No doubt, when these chains were gone, Jozsua would come looking to kill him. Dmitry was banking on it. One encounter could only lead to another between them. Dmitry forced his eyes open. Jozsua was back to watching him. His cheeks were flushed. The gorgeous blue eyes that had spent way too much time haunting his dreams held Dmitry's gaze. Jozsua's lips were parted on a pant. The desire to surge to his feet and kiss Jozsua was like a cheetah clawing at his spine.

Dmitry's fingers dug into Jozsua's back as he held the man in place and gave everything he had. When he felt Jozsua's muscles harden, he hollowed out his cheeks and took Jozsua down his throat. A gasp ricocheted through the room as hot cum filled Dmitry's mouth. Dmitry let it slide down his chin and run down his throat until he thought he might choke. He didn't care. It was the best way to go and—most likely—the least violent of his choices.

He swiped his face on Jozsua's stomach as he came to his feet. Jozsua turned his head away again, struggling for each breath with his face pressed to his arm. As tempted as Dmitry was to try to force the man to kiss him, he didn't want to force Jozsua to do anything at all. Jozsua was so much better willing and when he handed over control. Dmitry's stomach muscles clenched at the memory of Jozsua's eyes losing focus—the man's body relaxing into whatever twisted game Dmitry planned.

Dmitry fixed Jozsua's pants because all of this was his and he wouldn't be the one unlocking the chains. "We have unfinished business," Dmitry said as he dragged his lips down the column of Jozsua's neck. "I'll be seeing you soon." Without a backward glance, he left Jozsua alone. His body was hard and on fire, but physical discomfort meant nothing to Dmitry. It was his mind that sometimes terrified the hell out of him.

Chapter 2

At Jade's first stirrings, Josh did his best to get her dressed, fed, and out the door before she woke up Kip and Cameron. Nothing soothed him like family, and his head was so fucking dark, he worried he could level the world. Jade was so much like Kon. Every time she smiled, it warmed his heart. In those moments, he didn't feel as if he'd failed his brother on every level. His niece was alive, well, and happy. Kon would've loved that. Maybe, wherever he was, he didn't hate Josh for everything, including last night.

"We'll make a cowgirl of you yet," Josh promised, trying to focus on anything else as he led Kip's pony in a circle. Her tiny face was set in an intense line, showing her focus. Josh couldn't hold back his laugh. She was too young to be so serious. Someday, she would give men hell.

"I didn't hear you come in last night."

Josh glanced over his shoulder at Kip's words. Steam rose from the coffee cup between her hands.

"Ah," Kip said, as if she saw everything. "Judging by the dark circles under your eyes, you didn't come home last night. Good for you."

"It's not what you think," Josh said, needing her to stop. "I had business."

"That's disappointing." The grumbled words were obviously meant for Kip alone, but Josh didn't miss them. She moved closer. "You're allowed to have a life, you know?"

Josh nodded toward Jade "I have a life," he reminded her. "It's a damn good one and all I need."

"One day, she'll grow up and get married. What then?"

Keeping his back to Kip, Josh shrugged. "Then she'll have kids and I'll spoil them. I'll be everyone's favorite uncle."

A loud sigh rang out behind him. He knew then Kip wouldn't let this go. "I know, with Kon gone, things aren't the same, but Kon *is* gone." Kip paused. Josh held his breath. When Kip spoke again, she brought his fears to life. "If you want to stick around as Uncle Josh for the rest of Jade's life, her kids will be the luckiest kids on the planet. But, you know, there's nothing stopping you from finding him."

Josh's throat burned. She didn't need to expound. There'd only ever been one true "him" for Josh. The thing was, he didn't believe in coincidences and her suggestion coming on the heels of seeing

Dmitry was too much.

Switching positions, Josh brought Kip into his line of sight. He needed to see her face. "Have you ever heard of a place called Affinity?"

Oh, the guilt. It was written in her every line. She'd never been a good liar. He had her number. Kip knew it too because she didn't answer.

"When was the last time you spoke to Ryan and Max?" Kip's gaze danced away. She took a sip of her coffee. Kip didn't understand. He'd kept the truth hidden from her and now it was coming back for him. He bit back the words. They would bring her to her knees, and he couldn't do it, because some loyalties ran deep. "I love you," he said instead, because it was easier than spilling the secrets he held. Her gaze bounced to his and stayed.

Kip's features softened. "I love you too."

"Please don't do anything like that to me again."

Tears filled Kip's eyes, making Josh's nose sting. "I just want you to be happy. You used to smile all the time—just like Kon. My clown brothers. Now." She shrugged, looking helpless. "You're not you any longer."

That was because he'd died—murdered right beside his brother. By the man Josh loved more than life—the man who'd dropped to his knees at Josh's feet only hours earlier. The pain was too big. Josh couldn't hold it.

Without a word, he plucked Jade from the horse. Ignoring her protest, he handed his niece off to Kip. "I need to go." If she spoke, Josh didn't hear a word of it over the screaming in his mind. Heading out on foot, Josh pointed his boots toward the springs. If there was anyone still listening to his prayers, no one would follow. He couldn't be held responsible for his actions any longer.

*

If he'd been a good man, Dmitry would've walked away a long time ago. He'd done his job and taken out Konstantin Danshov. After that, he should've disappeared. Instead, he'd chosen the selfish path—the way he often did. When he'd been sent to infiltrate the Danshov family, he'd known—most likely—the day would come when his next order would be to slaughter them all. People didn't hire him for any other reason. No amount of forewarning could've stopped him from wanting Jozsua from the first moment he set eyes on the man. Since Dmitry wasn't a man used to being denied, he'd set out to have him. He'd fully expected to have his fill of Jozsua and still not bat an eye when it came time to pull the trigger.

Life has a sick sense of humor. He, who'd spent his entire life stoking his psychopathic tendencies, fell hard for Jozsua Danshov. Of course, as with all things when it came to Dmitry, Jozsua was more of a sickness. Still, Dmitry couldn't deny Jozsua had changed him. He was still a sociopath with psychopathic tendencies, but he also had an obsession, and that made a difference in him. The object of his desire was currently crashing his way toward some springs, looking thunderous. There was never a move Jozsua made Dmitry didn't know about. To his mind, it was ridiculous for Jozsua to hate himself over last night. He couldn't control his heart any more than Dmitry could. It was even more absurd for Jozsua to think he could run away from them—from what they had.

"You're as loud as the hell you bring."

A low chuckle escaped Dmitry. Jozsua's grandmother used to say the same thing. "I wasn't trying to sneak up on you."

Jozsua turned. Dmitry nearly stumbled. The impact of this man on his heart never lessened. His blue Mohawk caused the blue of his irises to stand out that much brighter.

"How did you find me?"

Dmitry bit back a sigh. It was as if Jozsua didn't know him at all. "I never lost you."

Only the flex of Jozsua's jaw let Dmitry know his answer hit home. Pain filled

Jozsua's features, and he visibly swallowed. "Don't let anyone find my body, okay? If you ever loved me, don't let Kipley suffer anymore for my family's sins."

He hated Jozsua a little in that moment. "Have I ever hurt you?" The question came out sounding hoarse, even to Dmitry's ears.

"More than anyone else alive," Jozsua answered, sounding broken, and without missing a beat.

Dmitry's face hardened. He felt it happen. If the man didn't want to believe in him any longer—so be it. "Turn around."

"What about Kipley and Jade?"

As usual, Jozsua thought of everyone but himself. "They have nothing to fear."

At his assurance, Jozsua immediately turned. The fact that Jozsua would take him at his word eased Dmitry's temper a hair. "On your knees."

One knee hit the ground, slowly followed by the other. "Are those the last words my brother heard?"

I will tell them how much you loved them. The words floated through Dmitry's mind. "No. His death was much different than yours will be." Because Dmitry would kill anyone who thought to ever harm his man. "Hands behind your back." The moment Jozsua complied, Dmitry zip-tied his hands together. He'd fully expected Jozsua would fight him. With Jozsua firmly secured, Dmitry moved to stand in front of him. Tilting his chin up, Jozsua met his stare. Pride rose in Dmitry's chest. An evil smile tugged at the corners of his mouth. Jozsua silently awaited his death, more than willing to die in exchange for his family's safety. Just as his brother had done.

"So brave," Dmitry praised as he took Jozsua's face between his hands. Before he could protest, Dmitry swept in and captured Jozsua's lips. To his surprise, Jozsua didn't fight him. Of course, Dmitry didn't try deepening their kiss either. He wanted to keep his tongue. Jozsua's lips opened over Dmitry's bottom lip, holding it.

"Kiss me for real." Damn. Only Jozsua could make him beg. "No one will—" Jozsua's mouth opened over his, stealing away Dmitry's plea. Darkness rose in Dmitry. This man believed Dmitry would kill him. Yet Jozsua still kissed Dmitry as if he loved him. What a damn mess they were. Black emotions overtook Dmitry's brain. Sometimes he thought he could hate Jozsua. Pulling away, Dmitry pressed his forehead to Jozsua's. For a moment, he simply stared into the eyes of the man he hated loving before straightening away. He couldn't stop the bitterness from coating his words. "I should kill you now for even thinking I could ever harm you. Fuck you for that." He stepped around Jozsua without looking back. "I'll let Kipley know where she can find you."

If Jozsua responded, Dmitry didn't hear it. The blood roaring in his ears had stopped all sound. It was best he left now before his temper demanded someone's life.

* * *

The anger sitting in his gut was a bad omen for the opponent facing off against him. Announcements filled the air. Odds, height, and weights were read. Josh didn't hear a word. Even the roar of the crowd was barely a hum. Kip wasn't speaking to him. It seemed finding him bound, on his knees and obviously accepting of his death, had been too much for her.

In all the years they'd known each other, he'd never truly been on the receiving end of her temper. If she knew the truth, would she even let him see Jade again? Josh cut off that thought before it took root. Instead, he embraced his rage and stared down the man standing across from him. His dark skin, shaved head, and large frame were a familiar sight. He'd fought Damarius Reed before—several times, in fact. They were both regulars at Warehouse District. They were evenly matched and about fifty-fifty in their win ratios. Tonight was different. Josh had murder in his heart.

The bell rang. Josh shot forward, landing a solid elbow strike and drawing blood before bouncing away. Point made. He was here to fight. Damarius came at him swinging. The first blow swiped Josh's ear, making it ring. A kick landed across his ribs with enough force to crack at least one. Josh accepted each blow, waiting for his shot. He had no intention of losing tonight. The pain soothed the beast raging inside him. He took everything Damarius had to offer. He fucking loved the abuse. Needed it. The first round passed with no clear winner.

The bell rang again, signaling the next round. While ducking the blows, Josh put his shoulder in Damarius' midsection, taking him down to the ground for a leg lock. Damarius fought back. Josh felt nothing. Adrenaline fueled him. A buzz rang in his ears. Tunnel vision set in. After digging his knee into the mat, balancing his weight, Josh twisted the man's arm at an odd angle, putting his strength behind it. He knew it wouldn't take much more pressure to snap the limb. He considered it. His demons screamed to be fed. Damarius tapped out, bringing the fight to an end and stealing the wind from Josh's fury.

Josh pushed to his feet, leaving Damarius on the mat. There was no such thing as sportsmanship in this place. At the end of each match, there was a winner and a loser. Nothing more. Hell, Josh wasn't sure if any of them were still human any longer. He let the official lift his arm in victory. He'd made some money. Not that he needed it. Nothing could lessen his rage. He should be dead on his feet. As he headed for the locker room, Josh ran through his options in his head. Something had to give in his life. He couldn't go home and pace the floor tonight. Josh needed... something.

After pulling on a T-shirt and a ragged

pair of jeans, Josh stamped into a pair of old work boots. No need tying them. They'd broken in long ago. Slinging his bag over his shoulder, he headed for the door. It wasn't always easy dodging all the freaks who got hooked on fighters. Tonight, all it took was one look at Josh's black expression to move them out of the way. He wasn't tempted. Not even a little.

Halfway to his truck, his steps slowed as he caught sight of Max and Ryan parked next to him. They stepped out when he moved closer. Both men wore matching serious expressions. Shit. He wasn't in the mood for this tonight. Lights flashed when he hit the button on his key fob, unlocking his doors. With his gaze averted from the couple, Josh headed straight for his truck. Max leaned against the door before crossing his arms over his chest, letting Josh know with his body language he wouldn't be moved. Josh bit back a growl. Part of him wondered if the men had a hand in setting him up. He couldn't believe they were there.

"Just hear us out, and you can go," Max said as if he could read Josh's mind. "Yes, I know you could easily move me out of your way," Max added, proving he was indeed a psychic.

"There's nothing to discuss."

"We're not the ones who will be doing the talking," Ryan said behind him, making Josh realize he was trapped between the men and their trucks.

Josh chose to play along. "If you're not here to talk, then why are you here?"

"To hear your apology."

In spite of everything, a burst of humor hit Josh at Ryan's claim. He cleared his throat to keep from laughing. "All right. This should be good." After tossing his gym bag in the back of the truck, Josh leaned against the side and crossed his arms over his chest. "Why do I owe you an apology?"

Max shook his head. "For the ass-chewing we got this afternoon from Kip."

A loud groan escaped Josh before he could call it back.

"It was brutal," Ryan said, adding his two cents.

"Serves you right," Josh said, deciding to brazen it out. "The three of you shouldn't have been plotting against me."

A line appeared between Max's eyes. "What are you talking about? We might be kinky, but we don't fuck on command. I'd never share what's mine with anyone we hadn't decided upon together and discussed beforehand. Yeah, Kip asked us to pass you an invite, but just to the club, not to go with us. That was all on us. Not to mention, you fucking stood us up last night."

Confusion crowded Josh's brain. He was also oddly flattered, but mostly confused. "But the way Kip talked... She knew..." *Dmitry.* The name floated through Josh's mind. *No.* It wasn't possible.

"Stood you up for what?" The deadly sounding and heavily accented question cut through the air, making the hairs on the back of Josh's neck stand on end. Ryan turned, and all eyes moved in Dmitry's direction. At five ten and one eighty-five, Dmitry wasn't a large man. There was something about the combination of his ice-blue eyes, deep voice, and the way he held himself that left people with no doubt they were dealing with a deadly individual. Even without knowing the things the man was capable of, Dmitry scared the hell out of people. He set off their inner alarms. In spite of his ten-thousand-dollar suit, Dmitry never left doubt in people's minds—he'd kill them without a second's regret.

Josh found himself shifting positions, coming to stand between Dmitry and his friends.

Dmitry's mouth lifted in one corner at the move, as if he knew Josh's thoughts. "Do you plan to introduce me to your friends, Jozsua?"

"No."

"Maybe we should go," Ryan suggested, proving he felt Dmitry's darkness.

Dmitry took a step forward. So did Josh. "Come now," Dmitry cajoled. "No need to run off. Shouldn't I at least know your friends' names?"

Josh didn't doubt for minute that Dmitry already knew their names. They needed to go.

Max stepped around Josh, showing a serious lack of judgment. "I'm Max. This is my husband, Ryan," he said, motioning toward where Ryan stood at Josh's back. At the introduction, Ryan stepped around Josh as well. He held out his hand, accepting Dmitry's handshake. Josh braced himself for anything.

"Dmitry," Dmitry said, introducing himself. "Jozsua was with me last night. If you were stood up, it's my fault."

Ryan and Max shook their heads. Max was the one who spoke up. "We're not offended. I can see how he'd be distracted."

Dmitry's smile turned sultry. Josh

couldn't look away. When Dmitry's gaze fixed upon Josh, his reaction was the same as it had been last night. He hurt. A flash of something dark crossed over Dmitry's features as his gaze swept Josh's body. He never looked away from Josh as he directed his words at Max and Ryan.

"If you'll excuse us, I need to check Jozsua's injuries."

Ryan and Max scrambled to get out of his way. Ryan tossed out their goodbyes. "Sure thing. We were just leaving. It was nice meeting you, Dmitry. Josh, we'll catch up later." Without waiting for a response, they piled inside their truck. Neither Josh nor Dmitry looked their way as they pulled from the parking lot.

Dmitry moved closer. Josh backed up until his shoulders were pressed against the door of his truck. Dmitry kept coming until he could push Josh's shirt up. He eyed Josh's ribs. They were already turning black. Before Josh could object, Dmitry prodded each rib until Josh sucked in a hiss.

"These are most likely cracked," Dmitry muttered under his breath. His gaze shifted, meeting Josh's. "Why did you let that man land a single blow?"

"I didn't let him do anything. It was a fight."

Dmitry's expression said much about his level of disbelief. "We have sparred too many times for you to pull that line on me. Why did you let him hurt you?"

Josh's mouth went dry. *I needed him to punish me for what I'm about to do.* The words floated through Josh's mind, but he refused to let them fall from his lips.

*

The answer was in Jozsua's eyes. He'd wanted someone to hurt him. Possibly he felt he deserved it because he still wanted Dmitry. Dmitry could see it all. Jozsua would never admit it. Moving slow as not to spook Jozsua, Dmitry gently cupped the man's jaw under the guise of inspecting the cuts on his face. He tilted Jozsua's chin down while moving in for a closer look. Without giving the man time to guess at his intentions, Dmitry swooped in and captured Jozsua's lips. Since Jozsua's bottom lip was slit, Dmitry kept his kiss light and to the corner of Jozsua's mouth. Every muscle in Jozsua's body was tensed to the point of snapping something. He was so rigid Dmitry couldn't move him at all. Still, the man didn't pull away. Neither did Dmitry. As far as kisses went, it wasn't the least bit hot, but it meant everything to Dmitry's heart.

"Those boys invited you to join them at Affinity last night, and you accepted," Dmitry said the moment he pulled away, because they needed to get some shit straight.

His eyes looked wary, but Jozsua didn't back down. "I'm pretty sure those *boys* are older than me."

"Both are thirty-two. They live at 3053 Garden Way Place. Next month, they'll have been married two years. The pair live a very active lifestyle. One that could get them killed." He could tell by Jozsua's expression that his threat hit home.

Jozsua being Jozsua, he refused to back down from anything Dmitry dished out. "Told you they were older than me."

Against his will, a smile pulled at Dmitry's lips. "Baby, everyone is older than you. That doesn't make them any less the boys I accused them of being.

Grown men pick a partner and keep their lawn fed and watered so good everyone is jealous of what they have. For those two, the grass will forever be greener everywhere they look. They're too busy plowing the neighbor's fields."

"Or they're everyone else's fertilizer," Jozsua said with a smile.

It had been so fucking long since he'd seen Jozsua smile. He'd only given Dmitry a small one. Mostly likely, his lip hurt too bad to smile too big, and—no doubt—he didn't realize he'd smiled at all, but Dmitry couldn't breathe at the sight. "They don't have what we do," Dmitry said. His voice had gone husky without his permission. The only time Dmitry wasn't in control of his every emotion was when Jozsua was involved.

"That's not hard," Jozsua shot back. "We have nothing at all."

At the challenge in Jozsua's tone,

Dmitry boxed him in with his arms. He kept a few inches between them. Just enough so he could feel Jozsua's body heat. "Is that so?"

Jozsua licked his lips. Dmitry's dick went hard. The lust lingering from last night and every other night since they'd been apart rose to surface, adding fuel to Dmitry's constant rage. "Say it again," Dmitry said, daring Jozsua to continue his reckless path. His blood boiled as he stared at Jozsua's mouth, waiting for the words to fall.

"Why are you here?"

"Because you are," Dmitry answered as he ate up the final inch between them. As their bodies collided, a sharp gasp escaped Jozsua, as if he'd been zapped by a Taser. He flattened his hands against the truck, refusing to touch Dmitry. Dmitry dropped his gaze, making a show of looking at Jozsua's hands. "That's too bad.

This body is yours and it's hard for you. You could punish me—make me pay for the way I've hurt you. Every inch of me is right here within reach, waiting for your hate." He met Jozsua's gaze again. Pain radiated from the man's stare. Dmitry pushed away from him. He couldn't hurt him anymore tonight. "But you've lost your chance," Dmitry said, straightening his jacket as if his erection wasn't messing up the line of his pants. He took a step away.

"I'm not like you," Jozsua said, bringing Dmitry to a stop. This time when he met Jozsua's gaze, all he saw was Jozsua's broken heart. It made the world seem less. When Jozsua had Dmitry's attention, he repeated himself. "I'm not like you. I don't hurt people just because it's expected of me." Jozsua swallowed and his expression somehow managed to become even more broken. "If the shoe had been on the other foot, I would've died before I hurt you or anyone you loved. You shouldn't insult anyone else's grass. Yours is dead." Without a backward glance, Jozsua jumped behind the wheel of his truck, leaving Dmitry behind.

Chapter 3

The day after Kon's body had been found in an alley, a key arrived by messenger. Josh had gone straight to the P.O. box, needing to follow every clue. Inside had been a single letter, addressed to him from Kon. His hands had shaken as he'd stared down at the familiar handwriting scrawled across the outside of the envelope. It was Dmitry's. In that moment, the full impact of the truth had slammed down on him. The only man he'd ever loved had murdered the only brother Josh would ever have. His grief had curdled into something indescribable, something he kept contained a little less every day.

The longer he'd stared down at the letter in his hand, the more the realization sank in. He couldn't read it. It was too hard. In his heart, he'd known whatever hid inside the inconspicuous creamy white envelope would change him forever. Josh had gotten in his truck, driven to the nearest bank, and locked it inside a safety deposit box without ever breaking the Danshov family seal. That letter had lived in the back of his mind ever since. The what ifs had picked away at his brain, threatening his already questionable sanity. What if Kon had known he would die? What if whatever had gotten him killed was inside? What if? What if? What if?

Now Dmitry was here and Jozsua didn't understand why or what he was after, but he knew it was time to open that letter. Knowing it was unavoidable wasn't helping. He stared down at the expensive creamy envelope, and his hands shook every bit as hard as they did the first time he'd seen it. An image of Dmitry floated through his mind. Josh cracked the seal. The letter slipped silently into his hand as if it had been patiently waiting. Josh's head spun, making him realize he'd been holding his breath as he unfolded the paper. Seeing his brother's handwriting again, after all this time, caused every muscle in Josh's body to seize.

Tornado,

Josh's eyes welled with tears as he read the nickname Kon had given him as a child. It was true. Josh had always possessed a hot temper and destructive nature, but Kon had always said it lovingly. Josh could almost hear it now. Damn. He missed his brother.

Tornado,

You'll never know how sorry I am for always asking too much, taking more than my fair share. You had this beautiful life with Dmitry, and I asked you to care for what was mine, leaving everything you loved behind. You should've hated me for that. Why didn't you hate me for that? Why didn't you tell me no? Was it out of brotherly love? Do you ever resent me for it?

Josh's gaze moved from the letter in his hand to the windshield. He didn't see a thing. Kon spoke as if Dmitry had nothing to do with Josh's decision—like Dmitry hadn't demanded he run. Like Dmitry hadn't been a snake in their midst. He couldn't think about those days or he'd lose his mind. Dropping his chin, he went back to reading Kon's letter.

My apology comes too late, I know. I also know it'll seem like useless words in light of what I must ask of you now. Once again, I must be the selfish one, always stealing life from you. First, don't let my Kipley fade away and stop living. With me gone, she'll have to be the mother and the father to our Jade. She'll need your strength.

Pain welled in Josh's chest, making it impossible for him to breathe. The first tear rolled down his cheek. Josh was powerless against it. He'd known. Kon had known he would die. The question had always plagued the back of his mind. The proof was in his hands.

The second part of my favor will be the hardest for you to accept. You are loyal. Sometimes, too much so. But, at the end of the day, you love Dmitry. He matches your strength. Your ferocity. In my heart, I believe he loves you too. So, for me, you must forgive him this. Even if he comes to you with my blood still warm on his hands...

Josh balled the paper in his fist, incapable of reading another sentence. Fucking Kon. Not only had he known he would die, he knew Dmitry would be the one who pulled the trigger. Yet, he still asked this of Josh. Kon was right. It was too much. He demanded more than his fair share. How dare he attempt to steal Josh's rage toward the man who'd betrayed him— who'd betrayed them all? The burst of anger passed as quickly as it came, replaced with a deep sadness nothing could fill. He flattened out the paper, doing his best to smooth away the wrinkles. These were the last words he had from his brother. Josh owed Kon enough to read them.

Even if he comes to you with my blood still warm on his hands, please know he begged me not to do this to you. He showed me pictures of Kip and her gorgeous belly swollen with our child and splotchy images of our daughter's ultrasound. Those images haunt me every second of every day. Dmitry has yelled, pled, and threatened me with permanent disability, but—in the end—this is my choice.

Drops of water dampened the page between his hands. His tears soaked through the paper, smudging the ink. Years of pain, anger, and helplessness overtook Josh. He'd moved from place to place. Hidden his accent. Given up willingly or had stolen everything important to him and Kon had *chosen* this. No matter how the words blurred, Josh couldn't stop staring at them, reading every single one. He had to know exactly how small and useless he truly was in the face of all the facts.

We knew this day would come. I know Kipley believes I've been setting up a new life for us. I have been, but it's a life for the people I love the most. One I won't be a part in. Someone has to take the fall for my many failures. I've held off the inevitable for as long as I can. One thing I will not do is cling to life and force the Danshovs to

81

punish everyone I love for my ineptitude. So I'm taking the deal—my life in exchange for yours, Kipley's, and Jade's. Dmitry can attest none of you knew any details of my dealings while in the US. I don't know if they believe Dmitry or if they fear him. Either way, I know he'll never allow them to go back on this deal. My life is over. I will not have you go down with me.

For a moment, Josh hated Kon for leaving him with all this. Red coated his vision. He'd chosen to leave them behind. It didn't matter he'd made the only choice he could. The fact that he'd escaped questioning by the authorities before being deported from the US meant nothing. The Danshovs wouldn't risk the possibility of it happening twice. Kon had gotten caught. His name was tarnished. No trails back to the family—not ever. The rage coating Josh's vision ebbed as Dmitry's name continued to stare up at him from the page he held. Josh needed to know it all.

As much as Dmitry has fought me on this, I'm certain he now wants me dead. He swears you'll never forgive him. Finding out he'd been hired to get the dirt on us was bad enough, but this, maybe he's right. Maybe I expect too much. The thing is, we're not normal, Jozsua. One day, I stepped out of a tattoo shop and into the path of the love of my life. It was as if she had been standing in the street just waiting for me. I latched on to the dream of Kipley with both hands and ended up destroying her life. She is beautiful and clean. She is a dream of normalcy and sinlessness— things I'll never be. We were born in the dark, and only darkness can hold us. I was just a fool with a dream. So don't walk into the street, Jozsua, expecting you'll find a normal life. You can't run from the one you have.

I'm sorry, Jozsua. It isn't enough, I know. Please make sure my daughter knows I loved her even though we never met. Don't be afraid to stand in a chair and scream it at the top of your lungs if she ever doesn't believe it. Love hard, baby brother, as I have loved all of you.

—Kon

Josh stared into space for so long he lost track of time and where he was. It seemed he should have questions. He should want to track Dmitry down and ask him a million things. Instead, Josh was just tired. His whole life, every time he turned around, everything was a lie all over again. It was exhausting. He wasn't sure he even had any fury left in him. Mostly, he just wanted to be still. Listen to music. Read a book. Have peace. There was a very real possibility that was exactly how Kon had felt. The only way he would ever know peace was in death. How sad for them all.

Blinking, Josh brought his surroundings back into focus. His gaze landed on G. Richards Bookstore. They had a coffee shop inside. Kip used to work there, and Josh had been there many times. It was a peaceful place. People bought coffee, sat, and read. It seemed serendipitous that it should be right there. His feet carried him to the door as if on autopilot. As he moved to push the door open, he realized Kon's letter was still gripped in his fist. After carefully folding it, Josh tucked into his front pocket before heading inside.

With a hot coffee in hand, he found a table in the corner and sat. The smell of books permeated his senses. He stared at his surroundings, still not seeing a thing.

Maybe he'd finally broken or something had shut down? All he knew was—he didn't want to talk to anyone or be anywhere. No place felt like home any longer. Nothing felt real. Back when Konstantin had lived stateside, they'd had a huge house in Texas. The place felt more like home than anywhere he'd lived before his father died, but never truly became his haven until Dmitry moved in. From that moment on, wherever they went was home because he was there. Since then, he'd been constantly sick to his stomach and drifting. Even the house Kon set up for them now didn't seem permanent. If anything, he felt like he was under Kip and Cameron's feet, and intruding on their life together. It was as if he no longer belonged anywhere or to anyone. He was alone in the world.

"What color is your hair naturally?"

Josh looked up from his coffee and blinked at McKenna standing over him. It was funny. For the longest time, everyone had pretended as if Josh was part of the background. Now, for no discernable reason, everyone was speaking to him. In this case, McKenna, the owner of the bookstore slash coffee shop where he currently sat, had spoken to him before on occasion. She wasn't one to align herself with rumors and general opinion. He waited until she claimed the seat across from him before answering her question.

"I am blond."

She nodded as if she suspected as much. "No wonder it holds the color so well. May I touch it?"

Josh hesitated, unsure of how to react.

"You may as well give in gracefully," a man in a twenty-thousand-dollar suit said as he slid into the seat next to McKenna. McKenna lit up by a thousand notches at the man's arrival. The way she snuggled against the man's side had Josh fighting back a smile. Josh had seen him before but couldn't recall his name. One thing he knew, it wasn't her husband, but even Josh had to admit the man's Italian accent was hard to resist.

"I'm not much on being touched."

McKenna snorted.

The Italian shook his head. His perfectly styled dark hair didn't move. It fascinated Josh. "She'll only wait until you're distracted and do as she pleases. I'm Asher, by the way."

Josh dipped his chin. "Jozsua." Josh winced as he heard his real name and thick accent slipping out. It was too late. McKenna's gaze sharpened. Before she had time to ask any questions he couldn't answer, he added, "Please call me Josh." Leaning closer, he gave in to McKenna's demands, hoping to distract her. "If it pleases you, then you may touch it."

While giggling like a schoolgirl, McKenna accepted his offer. "I'm a writer," she said as she ran her fingers through his hair. He hadn't known that, but then again, Josh hadn't bothered to care about much of anything. "I like the feel, smell, and taste of things," she added. "It helps me to describe them."

He hoped she never had a reason to depict him. "My hair would not taste good, I'm sure, but you are welcome to smell it." He flashed a devilish grin her way before he could stop it from happening. "I promise to avert my gaze from your gorgeous cleavage when you move closer."

A surprised-sounding burst of laughter escaped McKenna. "Another naughty male hanging out in my bookstore. It's like Christmas come early."

Asher chuckled. Even the man's laugh was ridiculously exquisite. "Where are your spouses this morning?" Josh asked, bringing the flirtations to an end. McKenna's husband was a fellow fighter. Josh respected him, and he didn't feel that way about many people. That still didn't mean he wanted to be friends, but he had some morals. Asher's eyebrows rose in question. Josh nodded toward the man's wedding band before he could ask.

"Ah," Asher said. "I thought perhaps we'd met before. Whenever I see McKenna talking to a man your size, he's usually from No Rival. The fighter community can be small at times. I'm usually better with faces, but I make mistakes."

Josh shook his head. "For a while, I did fight the circuit, but when Kip settled here, so did I. Now I fight underground—like McKenna's husband. The money is better."

"If you don't die," Asher said, proving he'd seen an underground match.

"There's that," Josh agreed.

Asher had a kind smile. He kept using it against Josh. "You said you settled here when Kip did. Are you a relation?"

"He's Jade's—"

"I'm Kip's brother," Josh said, interrupting McKenna before she made things awkward. McKenna's mouth fell open. Something about her surprise loosened his lips. "Soon after she learned she was pregnant with my niece, her husband unexpectedly passed away. Understandably, she needed a steadier life than traveling the circuit. She stayed with Brian and Terry until I got settled here."

McKenna shook her head, looking sad. "She never said a word. Like everyone else, I just assumed..."

Josh waved off her words before she could say anything to keep the rumors of him being Jade's father alive. After all, it wasn't as if anyone would believe the truth if they said it, but they needed new gossip to take root if Kip planned to keep both Cameron and Josh around. Plus, for Jade's sake, she needed to be able to openly claim Josh as her uncle. "You know Kip. She keeps things to herself. They were married for a long time and were very much in love. Actually, it could be quite sickening to watch at times. Anyhow, the grief was too much for her to share. Terry and Brian knew, of course, but she swore them to secrecy. She didn't want everyone's pity making her loss harder to bear."

Josh shook his head, feeling more honest than he had in a long time as he added, "Death does funny things to those left behind. Kip was willing to let people believe whatever as long as she didn't have to say the words. Sometimes simply shaping the syllables of someone's passing is the hardest thing in the world." Smiling, Josh tried to ease the heaviness of their topic. "Loving Cameron has eased her willingness to speak of it."

"Awwww," McKenna said. Her eyes welled with tears. "I still wish she'd said something. My first husband passed too young also."

A smile tugged at the corners of Josh's mouth. "She's a stubborn ass. No matter how I cajoled, she wouldn't open up to her friends. I'm just as bad. I don't like anyone enough to disabuse their beliefs that I'm a no-good bastard who dumped Kip when she needed me most." He paused as a hint of sadness crept into his heart. "Then again, maybe I am that person." But not for the reasons people believed. He tried shaking it off. "Anyhow, things are different for her now that she has Cameron. He's changed her."

McKenna's face lit. "I'm glad to hear it. I never see either of them anymore. Do you know how they're doing?"

Josh couldn't stop switching his attention between the pair sitting across from him. Even though Asher continued to hold his silence, it was obvious McKenna hadn't forgotten his presence at her side. Every few seconds, she would brush her cheek against his shoulder as if she couldn't resist. Asher drank his coffee, completely unconcerned.

"I do," Josh said, answering her question. "Kip, Jade, and Cameron have all come to live with me at our family's ranch. It's about an hour's drive outside the city. Jade has a pony now and is learning to ride. She's very happy and spoiled." As always when he spoke of Jade, Josh's pride shone through.

"You know, I've always thought Jade looks more like you than Kip. I always thought it was because...well, you know."

An unexpected smile exploded across his face. "She looks exactly like my brother." Horror crashed over Josh as he realized what he'd said.

"There's a brother too?"

Josh cast a desperate look around, searching for a way out. His gaze landed on a familiar figure sitting two tables over. Piercing blue eyes were fixed upon Josh, making him wonder how he hadn't felt Dmitry's stare. "He's passed as well," Josh explained, sounding distracted even to his ears. "Please excuse me. I have to speak with someone." Josh pushed to his feet and headed for Dmitry. The man held Josh's stare as Josh moved in his direction. Josh's mouth went dry. His heart beat faster with every step he took in Dmitry's direction.

"I'm finding you everywhere these days," Josh said the instant he reached Dmitry's side.

"You've chosen to notice me again. I've always been here... waiting."

Kon's letter burned a hole in Josh's pocket. Dmitry's gorgeous stare was too much. His brother was right. Even from the grave, Kon always knew best—they weren't normal. There would never be a day when Josh would meet someone on the street and fall in love—live happily-ever-after. He'd seen the underbelly of reality—been tainted from birth. Normal had never been in the cards. Not to mention, even if he met someone, there'd always be this man right here, as he'd said, waiting.

"Is this seat taken?" Josh asked, motioning toward the chair across from Dmitry.

"No." Dmitry sounded sad. Was this what had become of them? Would it always be this way? They were incapable of staying away yet unable to find a middle ground.

Josh sat. His gaze dropped to Dmitry's forearm. A rosary tattoo stared up at him. He hadn't noticed it before now. Until today, Dmitry had kept his arms covered with the expensive suits he knew Josh loved. Today's polo matched Dmitry's eyes and exposed some of the man's glorious ink. Without thought, Josh traced the tattoo's lines with the tip of his finger. Dmitry dutifully turned his arm over, allowing Josh access to the entire piece. He froze when he reached his name tattooed inside Dmitry's wrist. The font matched the tattoo Dmitry had on his side of Jozsua's name.

"This is new."

Dmitry's subdued silence was deafening. "Not to me."

At Dmitry's softly spoken claim, Josh moved on, tracing a line down the center of Dmitry's palm. His gaze remained locked on the man's hand. He had gorgeous fingers. Musician's hands. In fact, Dmitry played piano beautifully. He'd written haunting pieces. Josh had spent hours listening to Dmitry as he perfected each one.

Words flowed from Josh as if they'd been held too long at bay. "When you'd go away for the weekend for work, I never let myself think of where you were headed. Each time you came home, I never considered where you'd been." Josh kept staring at Dmitry's hand as he stroked each finger—lost to the memories. "I refused to think about what these gorgeous fingers had done while you were away. Where they'd been. Whose blood coated them. They were all bad people. There was no reason to ever think of them. That is, until it was my family's blood." Josh moved to pull away. Dmitry's hand closed around his, stopping him.

Dmitry didn't try defending himself. Instead, he leaned closer and brought Josh's hand to his lips. His hot breath fanned across Josh's skin as he simply held Josh's hand to his mouth without speaking. His light gaze held Josh's. Dmitry had always had a way of saying a thousand things without ever speaking.

"You forgot your coffee," McKenna said, setting Josh's cup at his elbow and breaking the spell.

"Who is your friend?" Dmitry asked before McKenna could get away. Since Josh didn't doubt for a second Dmitry already knew all there was to know about McKenna, he recognized it was Dmitry's way of letting him know he wasn't irritated by the interruption.

Josh pulled his hand away and motioned McKenna's way. "Dmitry, this is McKenna Travis. She owns this bookstore and is married to a fighter from Warehouse District."

Dmitry dipped his chin in her direction.

Taking a deep breath for courage, Josh waved toward Dmitry. "McKenna, this is my husband, Dmitry." Dmitry's satisfaction was a tangible thing.

The memory flared to life in Josh's brain, as if it had been yesterday.

"Is Dmitry even your real name?"

"Yes."

"What sort of contract killer gives out his real name?"

"The kind no one lives to identify."

McKenna snagged the closest chair and sat as if her legs wouldn't take her a step farther. Her gaze never moved from Dmitry's face.

"It's very nice to meet you, McKenna."

"Holy shit," McKenna said, sounding breathless and every bit as blown away as she appeared. Josh expected her to levitate at any moment. "That accent." McKenna made a humming sound. Josh got it. He'd felt that deep voice against his skin. McKenna finally glanced his way. "This is your husband?"

Josh nodded, incapable of saying the words twice.

"Damn, Josh. I never thought anyone could rival Asher in my fantasyland, but wow. You're a lucky man." She switched her attention back to Dmitry. It seemed McKenna didn't possess the same internal alarm as the rest of the world. In fact, a blush tinted her cheeks. The sight fascinated Josh. She was the most shameless person he'd ever met. He hadn't thought her capable of embarrassment. She shook her head. "I'm sorry. You must think I'm crazy."

A kind smile touched Dmitry's lips—

one he didn't show often. "Let me guess. You're an artist of some kind."

McKenna nodded, looking relieved. "I'm a writer."

"Ah," Dmitry said, pouring on the charm. "That explains everything. You're sensory driven. Do what you must, then. I can see that it is killing you."

Josh could only watch as McKenna flew to her feet. A bright smile stretched her lips as she moved to Dmitry's side of the table. She spoke too fast for Josh to catch every word as she inspected the tag of Dmitry's shirt, openly sniffed his collar, and asked questions about where he was from. She fired off the name of his cologne, proving this was something she did often. Dmitry showed the patience of a saint while answering her every question with a mixture of competent-sounding truth and lies.

By the time McKenna left them alone, Josh couldn't hold back the question any longer. "Have you ever told anyone the whole truth about anything?"

Dmitry held his gaze without shame as always. "No one still living."

Including Josh. Dmitry didn't need to say it. Josh was well aware he'd been fed many lies over the years. The saddest part was—the knowledge changed nothing. His eyes burned. It was the cruelest fate to love someone like Dmitry. Like he'd done thousands of times over the years, Josh wondered what it said about him that he didn't run for his life. Surely no sane person would know what he knew, see what he'd seen, and still want this cruel and calculating man. But here he was, forever trapped loving this empty shell across from him.

"Tell me to go away."

Dmitry's demand hung between them. Self-hatred rose in Josh's gut. No matter how hard he tried shaping the words that would send this man from him, he couldn't, and he hated Dmitry for it. Josh stood so fast his chair hit the floor. Without a backward glance, he walked away. If anyone stared at his abrupt exit, Josh wouldn't know. The only eyes he felt upon his skin were the ones that never went away.

*

Jozsua had willingly touched him. Held his hand. Called Dmitry his husband. It was insane to press for more. Dmitry had never been accused of harboring any such quality as sanity. The more Jozsua gave him, the more he craved. Because he'd found McKenna charming, Dmitry uprighted Jozsua's chair and threw his cup away before going after him. Timing acts to perfection was part of his job. He knew exactly how long it would take Jozsua to reach his truck and how long it would take for him to catch up. He waited until Jozsua sat in his vehicle, with his door still open, before slipping into the opening.

"Fucking hell, Dmitry," Jozsua said, gripping the steering wheel as if it was his sanity. "What do you want from me?"

"Everything," Dmitry answered without a qualm. "See me tonight."

Jozsua still wouldn't look at him. "I have a match scheduled."

"Tell me a time, and I'll meet you at the house. We'll go together."

"Not the house," Jozsua said, finally meeting his gaze.

Dmitry hid his wince. Jozsua didn't want him anywhere near his family. That didn't mean he would give up. "I'll meet you at Warehouse and we'll do something after you win."

He could see Jozsua fighting against his smile. "I need time to think about some things. You being here..." Jozsua visibly swallowed before starting again. "I never expected to see you again. It isn't your fault," Jozsua said, running his hand around the steering wheel as if he needed something else to do with his gaze other than look at Dmitry. "You tried telling me you were the devil. Yet I still fell in love with the angel you showed me. That's not on you," Jozsua repeated as he met Dmitry's stare once more. Dmitry wondered who he was trying to convince. "Tell me you're sorry," Jozsua demanded, completely at odds with his previous words. "Even if it's not true."

Dmitry didn't hesitate. "I'm sorry."

Jozsua's face screwed up in pain before he looked away again. "Now I want to know if it's true. I'm so stupid when it comes to you. My fight is at eight."

Dmitry kept his victory dance on the inside. Before Jozsua could shut him out, Dmitry snagged Jozsua's collar and held on as he covered the man's mouth with his. For the most part, the move had been a selfish one. He'd needed the pressure of Jozsua's lips against his own. The move had also been a calculated one. Jozsua was strong but led by his heart. Dmitry could threaten, beg, and make demands. He knew from experience the only way to budge Jozsua was to keep stealing the man's heart and use his love against him. Dmitry had to make Jozsua remember what life had been like with him before the world had gone to hell.

"Why do you call me Jozsua instead of

Josh, like everyone else?"

Irritation ran through Dmitry. He hated when people called Jozsua Josh. "That isn't your real name. When you're with me, I want the real you."

Jozsua's smile said a lot about how much he loved hearing Dmitry's explanation. "What about you? Is Dmitry even your real name?"

"Yes."

"What sort of contract killer gives out his real name?"

Dmitry's mouth twitched at the question. He didn't know why, but Dmitry found Jozsua's lack of fear over what he did for a living funny. "The kind no one lives to identify."

"Does that make me unique or do you intend to kill me one day?" The serious note *to Jozsua's voice gave Dmitry pause. It was scary how astute Jozsua was. Dmitry needed to marry him quick. Not only could he not live without this man, Jozsua needed the protection of Dmitry's name.*

"You're rarer than a snowflake in the Everglades."

The memory drifted away, but the words lingered on his lips once more as he trailed kisses along Jozsua's jaw. "Still my Everglades snowflake." The way the man's muscles relaxed at Dmitry's claim let him know Jozsua remembered too. He would win this man back.

Chapter 4

Whatever he did, Josh couldn't see Dmitry again without telling Kip everything. Josh wouldn't risk his family for anything with Dmitry. Never again. No matter what Dmitry did or said, Josh hadn't forgotten what it was like to learn the truth.

Open and half-packed suitcases littered the room. Josh stared at them. His breath quickened. His heart raced. Dmitry watched him, frozen, as if awaiting Josh's next move.

"Are you going somewhere?"

At his question, Dmitry tossed the clothes he'd been holding into a suitcase. "No. You are."

"Um. Okay. Where?" Josh could hear the barely suppressed laughter in his voice. He felt a bit crazed. Dmitry had never behaved like this before. He watched as

Dmitry continued tossing things inside the suitcase as if he expected the hounds of hell to tear down the door any minute.

He spoke as he packed. "You're going to collect Kip and then you're off to anywhere in the world you'd like as long as I don't know where you are."

Dmitry wouldn't look at him. Terror was quickly taking hold. "What are you talking about?"

At the panic in his voice, Dmitry finally met his stare. "I have to go after Konstantin."

"What the fuck are you talking about?" Josh repeated.

Dmitry circled the bed, moving to stand toe to toe with Josh. Every second that ticked by, the more his nerves strained. He'd never seen Dmitry anything but in control. The maniacal glint in his eyes had

112

Josh ready to fly apart.

Dmitry cupped Josh's face, as if attempting to make him focus. "I have to go after Konstantin, and you have to run."

The full impact of Dmitry's words hit. "Why would anyone send you after Kon? You work for him."

For a moment, Dmitry held his stare. His devastation was almost tangible. "No."

With one word, Josh understood everything. Konstantin had been under investigation for three years before his deportation. They thought they'd kept all the right people paid off to keep Kon in the country. Dmitry had shown up shortly after the investigation began, but he'd never been there to help. They were a job. All of them. A pain hit Josh in the chest. This was his husband. Josh couldn't breathe. He might never breathe again.

He'd been with Kip ever since, watching over her in any way she'd allow. It had taken him some time to convince her to move out to the mountain spring ranch with him. Not that he believed for a minute he'd been the deciding factor in the matter. For a while, it had seemed as if Kip was determined to forget Kon existed. It was true she couldn't let the outside world know she had a daughter with the famous Russian mafia hockey player. Everyone knew Kon's story. She'd never have peace. But, for a while, he'd worried she didn't intend to let Jade know anything about her father.

"I'm going to put you in a princess dress if you don't get still."

Josh bit back a laugh at Cameron's threat. He lost the battle at Jade's reaction.

"No." The loud wail rang from the walls

of the kitchen, and Jade dropped her fore-head on the kitchen table in the most dra-matic display he'd ever seen. At two, she already ruled their home. She also had more personality than most adults. In that regard, she was more like Kon than any-one he'd ever met. His little mini-Kon also hated princesses for some odd reason none of them had yet to discern. It worked in their favor when she wouldn't behave.

Kip had married Cameron two months earlier. The man was exactly what their home needed, which was something Josh never would've believed. As a cop and for-mer soldier, he was the opposite of every-thing they'd ever known. Yet, he fit. More importantly, he loved Jade and didn't deny her the right to love her real father. Kon was a part of their home. His office re-mained the same as it had before his death, and several photos of Kip and Kon scattered throughout the house. Josh couldn't have asked for more.

"Are you going to fight with the boys and me today?" Cameron asked, still trying to modify Jade's cranky-ass attitude.

Kip transferred a few of their lunch dishes from the table to the sink. "Are you sure you're okay to take her with you today?"

"Of course," Cameron said, plucking Jade from her high chair and setting her on his knee. "The guys love her and it wears her out."

Josh imagined it was also good for the men's morale. Cameron spent a few hours out of every day at a privately owned veteran's rehabilitation center. All the men involved were amazing people who'd come home from war with significant injuries. Cameron was one of those men. While serving in Afghanistan, Cameron had thrown himself on top of an Afghani child who'd been set on fire in the street. One side of the man's body was covered in extensive scarring, but it was nothing compared to what the experience had done to Cameron's mind. The child had not survived. It was a burden Josh didn't envy. Cameron had a definite human side Josh didn't possess. That was why Josh had to talk to Kip alone. He kept one eye locked on the clock. Time was running short, but he needed Kip alone for this. Even if she didn't hate him for Dmitry coming around, she might when she learned the truth. If that was the case, he wouldn't meet Dmitry tonight—simple as that.

When Cameron finally got Jade out the door, Josh nearly crowed in his relief, but still the words clogged in his throat every time he glanced Kip's way. She washed their dishes, and he dried. Side by side in silence they worked. Josh thought his mind might snap from the pressure. They rarely talked about Konstantin or Dmitry. It all hurt too much.

"I need to talk to you about something," Josh finally said, forcing the words out and leaving himself no other choice but to get on with it.

"Sure. What's up?"

"It's about Dmitry."

Kip turned the water off and gave him her full attention. Judging by the wariness in her eyes, it was obvious she thought he planned to rip into her over the Affinity thing.

"I talked to Max and Ryan. They won't bother you again."

Josh waved off her words. "It's not

that."

Her mouth lifted in one corner. "Things have settled down, Josh. You could run away with Dmitry and no one would ever know. There's nothing stopping you from reclaiming your life."

There were a thousand things standing in the way of his old life, but she didn't know that. He needed her to understand that. Reaching behind him, Josh dug into this pocket, coming out with the letter from Konstantin. "There's more to the story than you realize, and I can't move on until you know it." After taking a deep breath for strength, he unfolded the letter and held it out to her.

Kip eyed the paper in his hand. She backed away. "No. Kon meant that for you alone."

The truth struck him. She knew exactly what he held. "You know what this says."

She looked away. For a moment, Kip stared at the stove. "I imagine so," she said, sounding absent. Taking a step away, Kip waved for him to follow. Josh didn't hesitate to trail behind her down the hall. "The day after they found Kon, Terry took me to the hospital. He was afraid the stress of losing Kon would cause a stroke or whatever. When we got there, he fed them this bullshit line about my husband getting killed overseas in a car accident. I got a lot of sympathetic noises before they pumped me full of anti-anxiety meds. Then I was sent home with instructions to stay in bed for the remainder of my pregnancy."

Josh remembered. It had been a horrible time all around.

"Anyhow," Kip said, sounding ragged, "when we got home, I found this." Kip pulled a black bag out of a hidden compartment in her bedroom closet.

His eyebrows rose at the sight. Considering Kon had bought their house and picked out their rooms, he shouldn't have been surprised by any sort of modifications, but he was. Kip moved to the bed and set the bag down beside her. Josh took up position on the other side of it. He wasn't sure why, but he couldn't stop eyeing the leather carry-on-size piece of luggage. It was Kon's. Josh had seen it several times. It was as if Kon was in the room with them.

Once Josh was settled, Kip picked up with her story. "This was sitting on my bed when I got home, along with Dmitry," she added, sounding as if she expected Josh to take the news badly.

His muscles tensed, but Josh forced himself to hold his tongue.

Kip caressed the bag sitting between them as if Kon could feel it. Josh's heart squeezed in his chest at the motion. Kon had been his brother, but he'd been Kip's whole world. He couldn't help but wonder if that loss would ever ease. Even loving someone new wouldn't lessen all of the blow.

"What's inside?" Josh couldn't explain why he'd whispered the question.

A small smile touched Kip's lips. There was no humor or happiness in the gesture. "Kon," she answered, sounding broken. "Not him, of course, but everything that made him who he was. His wallet, cellphone, and watch. All his jewelry, including our wedding ring. Everything he carried and wore every day, including the day he died. There's also several pictures of

122

the two of us together, our marriage license, and information on every account he opened in my name around the world. None of us will ever want for a thing. On top of it all is a letter that looks exactly like yours and my guess is its contents are similar in nature as well."

Kip didn't open the bag. She simply kept stroking it lovingly as she spoke. "Dmitry waited patiently while I read Kon's letter. Afterward, I didn't react as I might have if I hadn't had quite so many drugs running through my system. But still, I cried and ranted. I may've even punched Dmitry a few times, but that part is mostly a blur. Dmitry took everything I threw at him. When the storm passed, he told me everything—Kon's thoughts, his last words. I cried some more."

Kip's eyes were red and filled with tears. Her gaze shifted over his shoulder as if she couldn't stand looking at anyone as she continued. "I fell asleep crying while Dmitry held me. The next morning, everything looked different. I hadn't realized how much my imagination was killing me—the idea of him on his knees in an alley, scared. It didn't matter if that's how it happened. Every time I closed my eyes, that's what I saw. That image ripped at my soul, Josh."

Kip sucked in a deep breath. It sounded ragged, pulling at Josh's heartstrings. "But he wasn't alone." A tear slipped down Kip's cheek. "If it had been anyone else other than Dmitry, Kon's last moments would've been different." Kip met Josh's stare. She looked more intense than he'd ever seen her. "Dmitry cared." More tears fell, but Kip didn't let them stop her. "Knowing Dmitry was there and Kon died on his own terms; those pieces of knowledge saved my sanity. He wasn't scared," Kip repeated, as if that fact meant more than any other. "Dmitry gave me that. I don't envy your position—between your husband and your brother. You're so much like Kon, funny and loyal. But just like Kon, you can also be stubborn and unforgiving. If you don't love Dmitry any longer, let him go. Set both of you free. Otherwise, you need to hang on to him with both hands and never let go. You only get so long on this earth."

Kip lifted the bag to her chest and hugged it. "You don't want to wake up one day and realize you lost your chance to have just one more day." After shifting to her feet, Kip shoved the bag back inside the hidden compartment and replaced the floorboards.

"What about Cameron?"

At his question, Kip flashed him a

smile. "I'll punch you in your dick, Jozsua Salko, if you ever tell my husband you married a hitman."

A roar of laughter escaped Josh at the threat. There was the woman who'd captured his brother's heart. With a loud sigh, Josh swiped at his eyes. "Oh God, Kip. I don't know what to do."

Kip chewed her bottom lip for a moment as if thinking the problem over or biting back words. Josh wasn't sure which. Finally, she focused on him. "What did Kon tell you to do?" He understood now. She hadn't wanted to ask.

"Forgive him."

She gave him a decisive nod. "Then you should, even if only to set yourself free."

Free. Josh wasn't sure if he truly knew the meaning of the word.

126

The tearing of skin as his opponent's fist hit its mark barely registered. Josh was used to pain. Equally, the sensation of blood running down his cheek didn't penetrate his adrenaline-fueled mind. Yet Josh knew exactly where Dmitry stood in the crowd. He was the only person not moving at all. Josh had spotted him the second he'd ducked inside the cage. Dmitry was such a strong force of nature; an empty circle surrounded him that people veered around as if he had a force field stopping them from getting too close. Dmitry had some silent power that went against nature. It had always been that way.

Sweat rolled down his back as he connected with the bag. Right punch. Left kick. Repeat. Left punch. Right kick. Repeat. He'd been at it for hours, trying to burn off the restless energy that had been building inside him for weeks. Josh couldn't explain it. He imagined it had something to do with eyes so light in coloration they were almost gray.

"Konstantin said you were some sort of professional fighter."

A chill raced over Josh's skin at the sound of Dmitry's voice. He grabbed the bag, stopping its swinging. "Years ago," Josh said, admitting something he rarely spoke of these days. "I was one challenge away from Heavyweight champ. Now, I fight underground."

A sexy set of light eyes fixed upon him, making Josh want more than he should or could ever have. "Why did you stop?"

Josh shrugged. He wished he hadn't confessed so much. "Heavyweight champ is a lot of publicity. I'm supposed to stay anonymous. So, here I am, back to being no one."

Dmitry's gaze dropped to Josh's bare feet before slowly lifting his chin and openly inspecting every inch of Josh's body. Every place his gaze landed felt scorched. "I meant, why did you stop your workout? I was enjoying the view."

A blush tried crawling up Josh's neck. He stopped it cold by force of will alone. Dmitry's claim was the last thing he'd ever expected the man to say. "I'd hate to bore you."

Dmitry's mouth lifted in one corner as if amused by Josh's comment. "Would you like a sparring partner?"

Josh eyed Dmitry's ridiculously expensive business suit. "You're not dressed for rolling around on the floor."

The small smirk exploded into the sexiest smile Josh had ever seen. He couldn't look away. "Have dinner with me tonight."

Josh blinked at the question. He wasn't sure if he'd misheard. He definitely didn't want to misunderstand. "I wouldn't want to take you away from Kon."

Dmitry's face screwed up in confusion. Even that was hot. "What is it you think I do for Konstantin?"

Josh shrugged. "He said hiring you would keep him safe and you seem..." Deadly, Josh thought but was incapable of saying it. "I just assumed you were some sort of guard. You're always here, after all." Watching me, Josh silently added.

A low chuckle filled the space between them, quickening Josh's breath. "I am no guard. Much the opposite, in fact. Maybe you should ask your brother what it is I do before you consider my dinner offer."

Josh licked his parched lips. He couldn't let Dmitry get away. "I'll go to dinner with you tonight if you'll spar with me tomorrow."

Humor flashed in Dmitry's gaze. "If you still want to go with me after talking to your brother, I'll be here tomorrow dressed to fight."

"Deal."

The bell rang. Josh's opponent came out dancing in circles for another round. Josh was tired of playing. Snagging the man's arms, Josh yanked him forward. Using all his strength, he leaned back before propelling his head forward, cracking the man across the bridge of his nose with his forehead. He went down. Josh stood over him, barely hanging on to his patience as he waited through the count. The idea that he'd known exactly where Dmitry was at all times wouldn't leave Josh. Kip was right. He needed to hold on with both hands because he was never going to shake Dmitry.

*

Waiting for Jozsua was the hardest part of the night. Seeing him get hit in the face and killing no one came in second. Rather than forcing Jozsua to search for him in the crowd, or giving the man an excuse to leave without seeing him, Dmitry chose to wait for Jozsua by his truck when his fight ended. By the time he spotted Jozsua weaving his way through the parked cars, Dmitry was grinding his back teeth with impatience. When he caught sight of Jozsua's face, every ounce of discontent slipped away. He recognized that determined expression. Dmitry could still remember the first time he'd seen it.

"Thank you for dinner."

Dmitry ignored his thanks. "Did you ask your brother what my position is with him?"

Jozsua's mouth quirked. "The weather was quite nice."

Dmitry bit back a laugh as he realized Jozsua's game. He wouldn't be ignored. "Gratitude is best saved for someone who wants nothing from you."

"My brother says you're a contracted insurance adjuster. My guess is that means you kill people for the right price. What is it you want from me?"

Without thought, Dmitry moved closer. Jozsua fascinated him. "You don't seem concerned by what I do. I want you in my bed."

Jozsua's gaze dropped to Dmitry's mouth before returning to his eyes. "Everyone I know kills people. Prepare to be disappointed. It takes more than dinner to lure me to bed." As if lending power to his claim, Jozsua turned away, heading for the stairs. "Good night, Dmitry."

"Does dinner buy me nothing at all?" Dmitry called at his back, hearing the laughter in his voice and incapable of stopping. "The night is young. I could take you to the movies as well."

Jozsua turned. His smile gave away his fight not to laugh. "What type of people do you normally date?"

No one. Dmitry had never been on a date in his life. He fucked people. That was it. "The kind of people who would at least kiss me," Dmitry said, because the truth was too crass for Jozsua's gorgeous ears.

Before Dmitry absorbed his intentions, Jozsua closed the gap between them and captured his lips. The overflow of emotion welling inside him rendered Dmitry momentarily useless. He was a puppet. Jozsua pulled the strings. When Jozsua *urged his lips open, Dmitry meekly obeyed. As their tongues met, a whimper escaped him. No one had ever caused Dmitry to make that sound. Desire. Lust. Need. Longing. None of those words were strong enough. If he'd ever wanted anyone else or anything else in his life, Dmitry couldn't remember doing so in the face of Jozsua. His kiss was gentle—like he savored Dmitry. The idea was more intoxicating than anything Dmitry had ever experienced. This man would belong to him. He couldn't accept anything less.*

With one final stroke of tongue on tongue, Jozsua captured Dmitry's bottom lip. Dmitry's lids felt too heavy as he savored the lingering flavor of Jozsua's mint on his tongue. Jozsua lightly sucked. Dmitry stiffened his knees as they weakened.

"This still doesn't make me like anyone else you've ever dated," Jozsua whispered

before turning away. "Good night, Dmitry," he said over his shoulder. All Dmitry could do was watch as Jozsua headed upstairs. Jozsua was more right than he knew. He was unique in every way to Dmitry.

Without breaking stride, Jozsua tossed his bag in the back of the truck before overcoming Dmitry. "Get in the truck," Jozsua said before capturing Dmitry's lips. It was a short but powerful kiss. It got Dmitry moving. He didn't understand Jozsua's mood, but he wouldn't miss his chance to have any part of Jozsua the man would allow. He jumped into the passenger seat.

"Where are you staying?"

Dmitry rattled off his address as his heart raced. Jozsua was intense tonight. The man had made up his mind. Now, all Dmitry could do was wait to learn his fate. Either Jozsua intended to ruin him for all others, which he'd already done, or kill him. Dmitry felt oddly accepting of either fate. He held still for the ride, refusing to fidget or give in to nervous chatter. God knows he wanted to. Dmitry craved the sound of Jozsua's voice. Not the fake and careful American accent he'd tried cultivating, but the real Jozsua. He wanted to hear about every second of every day he'd missed since Jozsua left him. Dmitry longed for past days when he would come home after a weekend of working and Jozsua would follow him from room to room, telling him everything he'd missed while he was away. Goddamn. Dmitry wanted his life back. His husband back. His whole life had been nothing but a series of pointless and unremarkable days while his years with Jozsua stood out in blinding flashes of color and light. Everything ached from missing those moments.

The drive to his cookie cutter, like every other house on the street, home was blessedly short. Dmitry had purposely stayed close to the places Jozsua visited most.

As Jozsua put the truck in park, he eyed the outside of the upper middle class brick home. "How long have you been right here within reach?"

"Always," Dmitry said as he slid from the truck. He pulled his keys from his pocket as he went, pressing a button on his key ring to disengage the security system. Before he could open the front door, Jozsua overcame him. For a moment, his chest hit the door and Jozsua's mouth opened over the cords of his neck, sucking lightly. The world spun and Dmitry found his back against the door.

Their bodies and their mouths collided. The back of Dmitry's head hit the wooden surface behind him in the assault. Jozsua's large frame ground against him. Dmitry struggled to suck air and kiss

Jozsua at the same time. The man's erection dug into Dmitry's hip. Dmitry's dick begged for attention. Jozsua's hand moved from where he clasped at Dmitry's clothes to between their bodies. His fingers shaped Dmitry's erection through his pants.

Jozsua rubbed his cheek against Dmitry's chin as if trying to give himself a beard burn rather than waiting for it to happen.

"Let me in, Dmitry. No one's touched me in so fucking long. I need you to touch me."

Nothing Jozsua said could've gotten Dmitry moving faster. He knew no one had touched what belonged to him. No doubt Jozsua knew allowing anyone to do so would be signing their death certificate. With him, that wasn't just talk. He nearly ripped off the doorknob trying to get inside. The second the door closed behind them, Dmitry hit the button on his keys a second time, reengaging the alarm before tossing the keys to the floor and dragging Jozsua down the hall.

He didn't bother with the lights when they reached the bedroom. Jozsua was already stripping off his clothes and Dmitry didn't want to stop to do a goddamn thing but Jozsua. Snagging the back of Jozsua's neck, he pulled the man forward before pushing him face down on the bed. He dropped to his knees at the edge of the bed, spread Jozsua's cheeks wide, and dove in face first. It was almost funny how he'd never had an ounce of interest in using his tongue on any man in any way before Jozsua. After the first time sucking this man's dick, Dmitry couldn't stop doing everything in his power to make him moan. The guttural sounds coming from the back of Jozsua's throat drove Dmitry to make it continue. He needed that sound. He tugged at his pants, releasing his erection as he ate at Jozsua's ass. Other than his spit, he had no way to ease this experience for his man. Just as Jozsua touched no one, Dmitry would never forsake a vow. No matter the lies he'd told, he'd meant every fucking word he'd said the day he married Jozsua.

Jozsua humped the mattress, openly seeking relief. Dmitry shot to his feet. He used his fingers to stretch Jozsua's asshole. The man was so fucking tight, he knew this would hurt him. As much as Dmitry didn't want that, he couldn't stop. His mind was too crazed.

"I'm sorry." It was the only warning he gave before pushing his way inside. A cry tore from Jozsua, bouncing from the empty walls of the room. Dmitry ground his back teeth and held still. His stomach clenched with desire. He didn't know how much longer he could hold back.

Jozsua pushed away from the mattress, holding himself up just far enough to jack his own cock. The move squeezed Dmitry's dick to the point of near painful. He couldn't move. Dmitry was already on the edge and the way Jozsua fucked his fist, milking Dmitry's dick with every pivot of his hips, had Dmitry ready to fly apart. He'd never met anyone more sexual. Jozsua could pull off positions, using his strength, flexibility, and stamina to his advantage, making Dmitry useless. It was addicting. He'd so easily cast a spell over Dmitry. Tonight was no different. All Dmitry could do was stand still while Jozsua fucked him—his body and his mind. Sanity had never been his strongest asset. If Jozsua made love to him tonight and walked away, Dmitry feared for himself. It would unravel him. He was already barely tamed. Uncaged, he might do anything. They'd have to kill him, putting him down like a feral animal, to make him stop.

Dmitry stared down at where their bodies met. He couldn't stop watching Jozsua's ass flexing as he fucked his fist while impaling himself on Dmitry's cock. His dick disappeared inside Jozsua's ass before reappearing. On it went. Over and over. He massaged Jozsua's lower back. His ass. Everything he could reach. His senses were on overload. Jozsua yelled his name and his ass locked tight on Dmitry's dick before the spasms set in. His balls drew up tight a half second before the pressure transformed into a blinding orgasm that rocked him on his feet. Stars popped behind Dmitry's closed lids. His mind was blank. There was nothing but silence and ecstasy. Wave after wave of pleasure crashed over him as Dmitry filled Jozsua's asshole with his seed. Even after collapsing into a heap, Dmitry couldn't stop riding the man's ass, dragging out every sensation. He could kill him right now and then no one else would ever have him. Dmitry shook off the crazed thought. He recognized it was just that. No way could he go on if anything ever happened to his love.

"You still have our bed." The words sounded muffled with Jozsua's face pressed into the mattress.

Dmitry rolled to the side. He sucked in a deep breath as his cock slipped from Jozsua's ass. "I still have everything," Dmitry admitted. "I could never willingly give up any part of us."

Instead of responding with words, Jozsua lunged. Dmitry found himself tucked beneath Jozsua in a heartbeat. For a moment, Jozsua stared down at him. He looked determined. Then his eyes fell closed, and he dipped his head. When their lips met, the oxygen disappeared from the room. It was their first kiss all over again. Dmitry was the puppet. The sweet stroke of Jozsua's tongue stole Dmitry's heart. Even though he'd never let himself believe he wouldn't have this again with Jozsua, he still couldn't deny the man's kiss soothed something inside him. Before Dmitry was ready to give him up, Jozsua rolled to his back, bringing Dmitry with him. Dmitry's eyes fell closed as they immediately snuggled into their normal sleeping positions. With Jozsua's heart beating against Dmitry's ear, Dmitry had to take a deep breath to pull the edges of his frayed mind together as a few insane thoughts tried sneaking their way in. Thankfully, Jozsua spoke and kept Dmitry grounded.

"I used to stare at my phone for

hours." Even though Jozsua wasn't speaking loudly, with his ear pressed to Jozsua's chest, Dmitry heard every word clearly. "You said you were going after Kon, but I thought... I don't know what I thought," Jozsua said, sounding defeated.

Dmitry knew exactly what he'd thought. "You expected I loved you enough I would never harm your family. In spite of all my lies, you trusted me to do right by you. I knew all those things." Dmitry stroked Jozsua's stomach, trying to memorize his lines. He fully expected, after tonight, Jozsua would disappear. "I know you won't believe me, but I tried." Jozsua didn't respond, confirming Dmitry's thoughts. His distrust didn't stop Dmitry from saying all the things he'd needed to say for years. "Konstantin was a good man. Maybe to the rest of the world that may seem a ridiculous sentiment. We know better. He was good. Life doesn't care about your wishes. It doesn't give a shit about your dreams or how you rant and rage against your fate. Life simply is. We're each handed what we're handed, and we deal with it the best we can. I wonder if we ever stared at our phones at the same time, wishing for one another," Dmitry said, changing the subject.

Jozsua trailed his fingers down Dmitry's arm in an absent gesture. "Every anniversary."

Dmitry smiled in spite of the topic. "Then, yes, we have. We have another one next week."

"What's the five-year gift?"

Dmitry kissed Jozsua's chest as he answered. "Probably something stupid."

Jozsua's fingers swiped through Dmitry's hair. "How did I let you convince me to marry you after only four months of dating?"

The confusion in Jozsua's voice pulled a low laugh from Dmitry. "I didn't leave you a choice. It was love."

"Was it?"

Dmitry's smile fell at the question. "It still is." Shifting to his knees, Dmitry straddled Jozsua's hips, pinning him to the bed. He needed to see Jozsua's eyes. "Maybe I've failed you, but I never stopped loving you." There was a hard edge to Jozsua's gaze that hadn't ebbed, even after their lovemaking. Dmitry glanced away. "You said you needed time to think. I realize I didn't give it to you. Maybe I should let you get dressed." He didn't want to give Jozsua space, but he didn't want Jozsua if he had to force him to be there. Dmitry went to move away. Jozsua's leg shot out, unbalancing Dmitry. While twisting at the waist, Jozsua snagged Dmitry around his and flipped until Dmitry was the one pinned. He stared at a version of Jozsua he'd never seen. Life had given the man much rage in the past couple of years.

"What happens if I stay, Dmitry?"

Dmitry's breath caught. Jozsua's question surprised him to the point he had no response. At his silence, Jozsua's expression hardened even more.

"What happens, Dmitry? Will I come home one day to packed suitcases, and you telling me you plan to kill Kip? Jade?... Me?" He stroked Dmitry's cheekbone. His eyes followed the motion of his hand. Dmitry couldn't stop staring at Jozsua's expression. Jozsua made it sound as if there was hope. "I want to trust you, Dmitry. Every word you shape with these sexy lips," he said, running his thumb along Dmitry's bottom lip. "I never know which are lies and what's the truth." He met Dmitry's stare. "You're such a sickness for me. I've already proven I'll accept your lies over anyone's truth. But I don't want lies anymore. Not even yours."

His heart pounding sounded loud in his ears. Jozsua seemed willing to give him a chance. "Would you believe me if I said I'd never lie to you again, even if I knew you'd hate what I have to say?"

"I would try to believe you."

Dmitry swallowed past the hope trying to rise in his throat. "What are you saying?"

Jozsua squeezed his eyes shut as if fighting with himself. Falling forward, he pressed his forehead to Dmitry's collarbone. His body felt tight enough to snap. "I'm saying, I hurt. I fucking hate you, but

I love you. It's not fair. Goddamn you, I don't want to spend another day feeling like this, but—when it comes to you—I'm scared of myself. I really don't know what I'll do if you ever hurt me again. Maybe I'll kill us both next time."

Chapter 5

Jozsua was sexy even when he slept. The sheer number of nights Dmitry had stared at Jozsua's empty pillow now contributed to why he couldn't stop watching Jozsua sleep. His lips were swollen from Dmitry's kisses. They were slightly parted on a breath and the desire to touch them had Dmitry clenching his hands.

The upper half of Dmitry's body was covered in tattoos. He dressed in business suits most of the time because he liked the way the expensive material felt against his skin. It was equally important for him to blend in, but Dmitry could shed those suits and don a T-shirt, exposing his ink, and blend into a different crowd. The ability to change like a chameleon mattered in his business. Jozsua didn't give a fuck about fitting in anywhere.

The man's blue hair matched his eyes,

making Jozsua exquisite. The only tattoo he sported covered one leg from ankle to knee. The rest of Jozsua was free of all ink. There were no piercings—none of the things a person would expect by seeing his hair. Jozsua's bulging muscles were beautiful and Dmitry wanted to lick them, but they weren't what turned Dmitry on. It was Jozsua's mind Dmitry couldn't resist. Jozsua was smart and strong willed. He was a man who knew his worth and demanded Dmitry know it as well. There was no better match for Dmitry in the world. There was no else for Dmitry—period.

Maybe I'll kill us both next time. Those words ran through Dmitry's head like a mantra. Jozsua's vow was further proof they'd always been meant to fall in love. They were so much alike. Anyone else might've ran for the hills at those words. Dmitry kept biting back a sigh. Only real love brought out that much crazy in people. Dmitry wanted Jozsua's passion. His rage. The insanity. No one else could give him what Jozsua did.

The temptation to capture Jozsua's lips was so strong it drove Dmitry from the bed. He wanted to watch his love all night, but if he stayed, Jozsua wouldn't get any sleep. That was not what Dmitry wanted. It was his job to keep Jozsua safe, which meant protecting the man's resting hours. Without any real destination in mind, Dmitry found himself standing in the center of his den at the opposite end of the house. His gaze landed on the piano sitting in the corner. He hadn't touched it since he'd sent Jozsua away. The piece was a bitch to have moved around the country, but he'd been incapable of giving it up. He hadn't been exaggerating when he'd told Jozsua he hadn't parted with any piece of them.

Dmitry pulled out the bench and sat. The black and ivory keys stared up at him. He'd kept it tuned for Jozsua. Music was the only thing about him still alive from his childhood, and only because he'd been taught to play by a neighbor. Everything else he'd cut out of his soul many years ago. People weren't born killers. They were twisted into them. The way Jozsua always looked at him when he played made him glad he hadn't given up this side of himself.

The keys gave way beneath his fingers and the years slipped away. Music flowed from him as if he'd played every day without fail. His eyes fell closed. Each note came to life in his mind. He automatically adjusted each one to suit his mood rather than any song he already knew. As always, the music was for Jozsua. For every time he'd been incapable of expressing how Jozsua made him feel, there was string of notes ready to fire to life. Tonight was no different.

*

Soft music pulled Josh from the soundest sleep he'd had in years. He reached for Dmitry. The bed was empty. The realization shook the last dregs of sleep from Josh's mind. A piano played in the distance. After finding his underwear, he followed the sound. At the opposite end of the house, Josh found Dmitry, sitting shirtless at the piano, eyes closed and lost in his own world as he played. Josh lost track of time as he watched Dmitry. He'd forgotten how amazing Dmitry could be.

His feet moved without his permission. The way Dmitry's shoulders moved in time with the notes he played hypnotized Josh. He didn't stop moving until his lips touched Dmitry's shoulder. Once there, he couldn't stop. He skimmed his mouth along Dmitry's nape before moving to kiss his other shoulder. The music fell silent. In its place, Dmitry's struggle to draw a steady breath filled the air. Dmitry tilted his head back and Josh found his fingers encircling the man's throat, holding him in place for his mouth's exploration. Josh's head emptied of all thought except for the taste of Dmitry's skin. He was in love with this man. No one else could hurt him the way Dmitry could. No one else would do for him but Dmitry. There was no hiding it.

"Play for me," Josh begged.

"Can't focus." The breathless note to Dmitry's voice didn't budge Josh. He needed this.

"Play for me. Please? I've missed your music. Missed you." A haunting melody rang through the room. Josh's heart skipped a beat. His tongue stroked Dmitry's pulse. "I love you," Josh said against the man's skin before he could call it back. The music fell silent as Dmitry twisted in Josh's arms.

"I'm sorry. Later, I'll play for you for as long as you'd like. Right now, I need you. I love you, Jozsua," Dmitry said, pulling Josh in for a kiss. "So goddamn much," he added as he claimed Josh's mouth.

"Come back to bed," Josh begged between kisses. If Dmitry didn't intend to keep playing, Josh needed to hold him. Maybe one day soon he'd be over this gnawing emptiness plaguing him, but it wouldn't be tonight.

Dmitry shot to his feet, bringing Josh with him. "Anything you want."

"Anything?" Josh taunted, brushing

his lips across the shell of Dmitry's ear as he followed him down the hall. "Are you sure you want to stick with that word?"

An evil-sounding chuckle rumbled from Dmitry's chest. "I'm not intimidated by the idea."

"One day soon I'll test that theory," Josh promised. "Right now, I really want to cuddle." Josh matched Dmitry's steps while holding on to the man's hips. He knew he was making the trek from one end of the house to the other take longer, but he didn't want to let go. "Naked, of course," Josh added, in case Dmitry thought he wasn't open to taking their cuddling up a notch. Dmitry could be damnably literal when he put his mind to it.

"Is there any other way?" Dmitry asked, sounding genuinely curious.

Not if Josh could help it. He'd never craved bare skin against his body so badly in all his life.

*

A plate of sliced fruit stared at Josh when he finally lifted his heavy lids. For a moment, he blinked at the chunks of red, yellow, and orange before his mouth pulled at the corners. Old hurts and anger tried pushing their way in with the morning light. Hope and happiness was damnably hard to beat into submission. Kip and Kon had both been adamant in their defense of Dmitry. Josh's love latched on to any thread of an excuse to burst to life. Josh couldn't tear his gaze away from the plate beside him. It was just fruit, but Josh's throat squeezed. A plate of food was so Dmitry. It was the small things he'd lost when Josh had lost the love of his life. No one took care of him. No one ever would—

not the way Dmitry did.

Scooting up the bed, Josh settled against the headboard. After snagging the plate, he popped a piece of pineapple into his mouth. It was delicious. A napkin sat on one corner of the plate. Josh unfolded it and a tiny piece of paper slipped out.

I love you.

Josh stared down at the three words scratched out on the paper. He set the fruit aside. Food could wait. Before going in search of Dmitry, Josh dipped into the bathroom and splashed cold water on his face. He didn't have a toothbrush or a change of clothes. Josh rinsed with mouthwash and slipped into last night's clothes. He'd have to run home and grab a shower before making any plans for the day.

Dmitry's house was bigger in the daylight. The night before, Josh had been intent on finding the bed and then only ventured out to find where Dmitry kept his piano. Now, with the house silent, the search for Dmitry had Josh taking an unintentional tour. He found the kitchen first. It was a light shade of yellow with granite and steel everything. Since Dmitry was an amazing cook, Josh wasn't surprised to see the kitchen was beautiful. No doubt, Dmitry spent a lot of time there. Josh could picture him, standing at the stove—shirtless with a hand towel draped over one shoulder. Damn, Josh missed watching Dmitry cook. Since the kitchen was empty, Josh moved on to the living room. It was a little less extravagant. A soft-looking burgundy sofa sat against one wall while a flat screen TV hung from the other. There wasn't a coffee table. In fact, the room didn't invite people to linger. The room was also empty of Dmitry's presence.

Across from the front door, a staircase

led to the unknown. Josh continued past the stairway, determined to finish exploring the downstairs first. On the other side of the stairs, a second hallway led to two rooms—the den where he'd found Dmitry playing the piano the night before and an office. The instrument sat silent, so Josh didn't bother with that room. Instead, he headed for the office. Tall bookshelves lined the walls and an oak desk took up one half of the room. Two uncomfortable-looking antique chairs sat facing one another. Josh recognized them as his grandmother's. It was odd how much of the furniture had been in their home before their split. The bedroom furniture was all the same. Nostalgia washed over Josh. The room smelled like Dmitry—leather and spice. In that moment, Josh wanted his life back with a desperation he hadn't experienced in years.

Dmitry's arms encircled Josh's waist.

He hadn't heard the man come in behind him, but he also didn't jump in surprise. It was as if the encounter fit—like they should touch unexpectedly in every room of this house, because that was what married people did. Tears pressed at the backs of Josh's eyes. His nose burned. This was his goddamn life, and it had been sitting here, in stasis, just a short drive away—waiting. Even as Dmitry's lips touched Josh's neck, Josh couldn't speak. The feeling, as if Dmitry had placed a bookmark in his life, holding his place, had Josh ready to break down.

Josh nodded toward one of the chairs, trying to get himself under control. "My nana used to sit in that chair. I would climb in her lap and she would sing to me."

"Probably while smoking a pipe," Dmitry said on a chuckle, proving how well he knew Josh's family. "She was completely mad like that." His hold tightened. "Did you sleep okay?"

Josh couldn't hold it in. "Apparently, I've missed our bed even more than I realized, because I think I died."

Dmitry somehow managed to snuggle even closer. "If it's any consolation, our bed has missed you too. It creaks and groans every night as I toss and turn without you. I know it's probably too soon for you to even consider it, but—"

Josh's cellphone rang, cutting off Dmitry's question. It was Kip's ringtone. Josh didn't hesitate to dig the device from his pocket and answer.

"Hello?"

"Hey, Josh. I'm sorry to bother you, but I took Jade to daycare this morning so I could go to my hair appointment. No sooner than they got half my hair in foil, the center called and said Jade is running a low-grade temp and needs someone to pick her up. Cameron can't leave work without someone to cover his area, and there's no one."

"I'll go get her," Josh offered before Kip could ask.

"Thank you. I hate cutting into your plans, but I can't leave here."

"It's not a problem. I can't have my monster suffering."

Kip sighed. "Thank you. I'll get out of here as quick as I can."

Josh shook his head, already searching for his keys with Dmitry following in his footsteps. "Don't bother. It's just me. I didn't have any plans."

"Thank—"

It was Josh's turn to sigh. "If you thank me again, I'll hang up on you," Josh said, cutting her off.

Kip snorted at his threat. "For your information, I need to go anyhow."

"Love you too," Josh said. Laughter laced his words, but he meant them. He hung up on Kip before she got the chance. Josh already knew that would be her next move. The instant he was free of Kip, the disappointment set in. He honestly didn't mind being the uncle for the day, but it meant his time with Dmitry was over. Back to reality. "Jade is sick. I need to pick her up from daycare."

A line appeared between Dmitry's eyes. "Why is she in daycare?"

Josh shrugged. "Kip wants her to have a normal life—friends and a head start on school, so she put her in a pre-school two days a week for now. Plus, it gives Kip a chance to do adult things without hunting down a babysitter. Anyhow, she's running a fever, and Kip is at the hairdresser. It's not that far from where you left your car. If you'd like, I'll drop you off on the way."

Dmitry wasn't one for nervous gestures. He never shifted his weight or chewed his bottom lip. Josh got the impression, if he did those things, he'd be doing it now. The way he watched Josh, as if expecting rejection, pulled at Josh's heartstrings. "I could go with you to get Jade."

"What about your car?" Josh asked to give himself a minute. Dmitry was casual today. His T-shirt and jeans made Josh's mouth water. It meant Dmitry hadn't planned on leaving the house. It also gave Dmitry a human edge Josh couldn't resist. Part of him wanted to say no. Most of him wanted to let Dmitry have anything he wanted.

"It's locked safely in the garage."

Dmitry's answer effectively distracted Josh. "How did you pull that off?"

"I never drive to Warehouse District. No way in hell would I leave a vehicle unattended in Conti territory."

Josh's mind went blank. Sometime in the past few years, his life had normalized a hair. He hadn't heard anything referred to as territory since Konstantin's deportation. "What?"

Dmitry nodded. "I assumed you knew. All underground matches in every major city are run by the local mafia. In the case of Vegas, this is Conti territory. You know, given my profession, I have to watch my back. I wouldn't put it above anyone to try to take me out." It was ridiculous for Josh to feel blindsided, but he did. He hadn't realized how much he enjoyed the blissful state of ignorance until he was basking in knowledge. Dmitry wouldn't stop feeding it to him. "That's why your father started you out so young, teaching you how to fight. It had nothing to do with survival. Boris ran the underground back home. I imagine he thought he could make a lot of money off you. That's why Konstantin was

169

so quick to bring you here the moment Boris died. He didn't mind if you chose to fight, but he didn't want that life thrust upon you—being forced to take a dive when ordered. Winning only when it suited your father's purposes and lined his pockets. It's the way of the world."

Josh could've gone his whole life without knowing any of that. He felt sick. Was that how Warehouse District was run? Had he earned every win or were the bets rigged? Jesus. His phone beeped, signaling an incoming text message and saving Josh from his spiraling thoughts.

Kip: *I forgot you don't have a car seat. Stop by Styles by Genie on the way to the center and grab mine out of my car.*

Josh: *On it.*

"I have to get Jade," Josh said, grasping for any sense of reality. He glanced up from his phone, catching the disappointment in Dmitry's expression before he hid it behind his usual mask. It wasn't Dmitry's fault Josh had been born into a crazy mess. Not to mention, Josh really didn't want to say goodbye yet. "I know how you hate leaving the house in jeans. If you want to change, I can wait."

Dmitry's accent thickened when he spoke, proving how moved he was by Josh's offer. "A sick baby is waiting on us. I'll survive people seeing me slumming it."

Without thought, Josh moved closer. He held Dmitry's gaze as the space between them disappeared. "I love you." His insides shook at the thought of letting Dmitry into Jade's life. "She's just a baby."

Dmitry's mouth lifted in the kindest smile Josh had seen in a long time. "Yes, and you trust me more than you're admitting. Otherwise, you wouldn't be here at all."

Josh kissed him because he didn't know if it was true and he didn't want to admit it. Kissing Dmitry was so much easier than saying the words. If Dmitry let him down again, Josh was scared of what he might do.

*

Jade's little cherub face was blood red with fever by the time they reached the daycare. The way Jozsua had chewed his bottom lip in worry as they drove out to the ranch had Dmitry on edge. He didn't spend time with children, but he knew they were resilient. Other than the reddened skin, Jade looked fine. In fact, she was perfectly content sitting next to Dmitry on the couch with her feet in his lap, watching him as if she expected him to do something to entertain her. Of course, that could've been due to him pretending to pull off her toes and eat them every time Jozsua looked away. She wasn't laughing, but she'd made a point of kicking off her shoes and keeping her feet

172

where he could get to them.

"Kip says there's some fever reducer in the cabinet," Jozsua said, coming to his feet. "I'll see if I can find it."

Dmitry played innocent while Jozsua eyed him. "Okay."

"Do you want me to take Jade with me?"

Dmitry shook his head. "We're fine."

The second Jozsua was out of sight, Dmitry was back to playing with Jade's tiny toes. "What's your name?"

Dmitry blinked in surprise at Jade's adult-sounding question. "It's Dmitry. Why are you grown?"

She giggled. It was adorable.

Jozsua reappeared, medicine in hand. "These dosage instructions are ridiculous." He unscrewed the lid. "Never mind. The little dropper thing is marked." He glanced up and looked back and forth between them as if trying to figure out what he'd missed.

Jade pointed at Dmitry. "Tree is silly."

Jozsua's mouth twitched. "Is he now? I don't think anyone has ever described Tree as silly." Jozsua choked on the name. Dmitry bit the inside of his cheek to keep from laughing. "Look, girlie. You have to take this stuff. It says it tastes like bubble gum." He sniffed it. "It smells good."

She dutifully opened her mouth without a fight. Dmitry was impressed.

"Do you want something to drink?" Dmitry asked, just in case it didn't in fact taste like bubble gum.

Jade rolled from the couch and headed for the kitchen. "I'll get it."

With a snort, Dmitry met Jozsua's laughing gaze. "Why is she grown?"

He shook his head. "She has her dramatic days, but—for the most part—she got Kon's temperament." Jade padded back into the living room, juice box in hand. She passed it to Dmitry before climbing into his lap and reclaiming her juice. She yanked at the straw, trying to pull it from the plastic without much luck. Dmitry fixed it for her. He intentionally didn't look Jozsua's way. The man's stare bored into Dmitry's skin. With Jade settled into his hold and happily sucking down her drink, Dmitry finally chanced a glance at Jozsua. They held each other's stare. Neither of them showed an ounce of emotion, but there was so much between them unsaid.

Jade's weight increased in his arms. Her juice box fell, pulling Dmitry's attention her way. She was asleep. He shifted her in his arms so she'd be more comfortable before settling in for a long haul. Even though she hadn't cried or complained, it was more than obvious Jade didn't feel good. He hated to wake her.

"This is what I wanted for us," Jozsua

said, snagging Dmitry's focus once more. A self-deprecating smile touched Jozsua's lips. "It's crazy, I know. You being who you are and me coming from where I do, the thoughts should've never crossed my mind." He held Dmitry's stare while Dmitry didn't draw a single breath. "But they did," Jozsua added. "All the time. Stupid, huh?" Before Dmitry could rub two brain cells together and decide how he felt, Jozsua shifted to his feet. "I'll go put this up," he said, motioning toward the medicine before making an obvious run from the heaviness of their topic.

Dmitry carefully stood and transferred Jade into the spot he'd vacated. After making sure she wouldn't budge, he covered her with a blanket he found folded up on the loveseat. For a moment, he stood still, watching her sleep and wondering what to do. He knew next to nothing about kids. Would she roll off and hurt herself? There wasn't a coffee table, and the couch wasn't that tall. It was possible, if she did fall, it would only piss her off. With his inner pep talk out of the way, Dmitry went in search of Jozsua. He found the man leaning against the kitchen sink and staring at nothing. His eyes were unfocused as if lost in thought.

Dmitry closed the distance between them. Every inch. He captured Jozsua's lips and stole the man's kiss without giving Jozsua a say in the matter. Having his husband's tongue stroking his own broke the words loose in Dmitry's throat.

"I can give you any life you choose," Dmitry said as he changed angles. For a moment, he enjoyed the sensation of Jozsua's light touch and the taste of his love before pulling away and holding Jozsua's gaze. "It doesn't matter who I am or where you came from. If you want this life, you'll have it. Say the words, and I'll give you anything."

The back door swung open and Cameron stepped in. His gaze swept the room, seeing everything, while his expression gave away nothing. Dmitry took a step back. He hated giving up touching his husband, but neither would he put Jozsua on display. Cameron closed the door behind him before crossing the room with his hand outstretched.

"You must be Dmitry. Kip told me all about you."

Dmitry accepted the man's handshake. "You must be Cameron."

"You can call me Cam," Cameron said, taking a step back. He focused on Jozsua. "I found someone to cover my patrol and got an appointment for Jade at the doctor."

Dmitry motioned toward the living room. "Jozsua gave her something for the fever. She is sleeping on the couch."

Cameron dipped his chin. "I appreciate that," he said as he headed for the living room, leaving them alone once more.

Once he was gone, Dmitry met Jozsua's stare. The man's eyes blazed with unnamed emotion. "One of these days, we'll get to have five minutes of serious conversation without interruption."

A smile exploded across Dmitry's face. "Probably not today."

"Yeah," Jozsua said, sounding put out and making Dmitry laugh.

He linked his fingers through Jozsua's and tugged. "Come on. Let's go see if Cameron needs any help."

Jozsua allowed himself to be dragged along. "Should I warn Cam there's no way in hell you'll ever call him by anything other than Cameron?"

Dmitry bit his lip to keep from laughing. It took everything he had to hide the laughter in his voice. "Don't. It'll be fun to see how long it takes for him to notice and how long after that for him to become annoyed."

"You're hopeless."

He was, but not in the way Jozsua meant. Dmitry was hopelessly in love with Jozsua.

* * *

Night had always been Josh's favorite part of the day. He loved everything about it. The stars twinkled, making him feel small, but also as if he could ask for anything he wished. The night sky was proof there was something or someone powerful enough to create such beauty. Therefore, they'd have no trouble granting the silent favors he begged.

The phone Josh kept balanced on his knee vibrated a half second before the face lit. He knew before he looked away from the sky and down at his phone who it would be.

Dmitry: *Will I see you tonight?*

Josh: *I'm not sure.*

Dmitry: *I can come to you, if you'd like.*

Josh: *I miss you.*

Dmitry: *Is that your answer?*

Was it? Was the fact that he missed Dmitry the only real answer he needed? No. Josh knew exactly what held him back. Dmitry had married him. The man had gotten down on one knee and begged Josh to spend the rest of his life with him. He'd spoken his vows in front of Josh's family and God. The whole time, he'd been lying about the most basic thing—why he was in Josh's life in the first place. It felt like the deepest of betrayals.

Now, Josh had questions and only one person had answers. Josh didn't fully accept, until he'd driven an hour across town to Dmitry's house, that he trusted Dmitry would tell him the truth if only

Josh would ask. The front door opened before Josh had time to knock. Dmitry stood in the doorway, wearing nothing more than a pair of dress slacks unbuttoned at the waist. His feet were bare. For some reason—one Josh couldn't explain—that detail made Dmitry feel more like the man Josh had married than anything had before now.

He didn't bother saying hello. "I can't take the lies sitting between us."

Dmitry took a step back, letting Josh in. He didn't look surprised by Josh's words. Perhaps he'd even been waiting for Josh to say them. Dmitry closed the door behind Josh.

"I never expected to love you," Dmitry said the moment they were closed away from the world. Josh's feet froze to the floor at the admission. It seemed ridiculous now. In spite of everything, this was his husband. Josh knew him. The man was a killer—never meant to love anyone, but that had always been part of the appeal. Dmitry had always made Josh feel powerful, because he was the seed of love Dmitry shouldn't have, but he did. Now he stared at the man he loved and waited, because if Josh knew nothing else, he knew Dmitry would tell him the truth.

Dmitry didn't disappoint. "Then, one day, I did," Dmitry added, looking proud of the words leaving his lips. "I'd never thought myself capable of feeling anything at all. Those things had been stripped of me at a very young age by monsters. One night, I looked at you, and this pressure built in my chest. I found myself hoping we both lived to be a grand old age and that you would outlive me because I didn't want to be left behind without you. More than that," Dmitry said, sounding fierce. "I wanted to reach inside myself and cut out this dark disease living in me, corrupting me." Dmitry's face continued to harden, becoming almost inhuman. "Now I see myself as I truly am. Evil isn't a part of me I can cast away. I was born bad—a rotted soul."

The backs of Josh's eyes burned. He couldn't deny having similar thoughts about Dmitry, but it hurt hearing Dmitry say such things about himself. Even if there was nothing human about Dmitry, that didn't stop Josh from loving him. What did that say about Josh?

Dmitry's eyes snapped into focus, as if coming back to himself. Shoving his hands in his pockets, Dmitry leaned his shoulders against the wall and focused on Josh. With the darkness of the foyer surrounding them, it seemed the perfect spot to spill their secrets.

"I fed the Danshovs every lie and bit of misinformation I could, hoping to keep them at bay. In hindsight, I realize there was no keeping the wolves from our door forever. It's funny how love and hope can blind you from reality. Once we were married, you were off limits to them and they knew it. At first, that felt like a win." The way Dmitry held Josh's gaze, as if he needed Josh to really listen to him, had Josh hanging on every word. "When they ordered Konstantin's death, the thought of actually killing him never crossed my mind. I was so damn certain I could find a way to keep him alive." A self-deprecating smile touched Dmitry's lips. "You were right when you said if the shoe was on the other foot, you never would've hurt me like I did you. You have to know I would not have done that to you if life had given me a single fucking way out." The desperation in Dmitry's voice almost broke Josh.

He felt the same as he had the night he'd learned Dmitry had killed Konstantin. This time, it was for a different reason.

185

Losing two years of his life, for things neither of them could control, deserved some recompense. Josh wanted his payment in blood and destruction. Dmitry straightened away from the wall and took a step toward Josh. Josh's mouth went dry at Dmitry's expression. For the millionth time, Josh wondered if Dmitry could read his mind. The dark hunger flashing in Dmitry's eyes matched Josh's rage. Black emotions built inside Josh until he worried his skin would rip apart. He needed an outlet for his rage. The idea of physically harming Dmitry in any way made his stomach churn. There was only one option. He bit his lip until he tasted blood, trying to hold back the words. Dmitry moved closer—like a wild animal, pacing and waiting to pounce.

The demand ripped from Josh's throat on a growl. "Hurt me, Dmitry. Punish me."

As if Josh had given him exactly what

he needed, Dmitry sprang. Josh's clothes disappeared in a frenzy of motion. In one quick move, Dmitry hooked Josh's ankle and shoved, taking Josh to the floor. His head hit the hardwood surface of the entryway with so much force that Josh saw stars. Dmitry's teeth sank into his chest, hard enough to break the skin. The moans tearing from Josh's throat were out of his control. If Dmitry was a rotted soul, Josh was the picture of perversion. He wanted Dmitry to fuck him so hard it hurt—make him bleed and beg. Josh hated Dmitry. He also loved him more than life.

The raging desire to kiss Dmitry softly even as Dmitry tore away his skin was pressing on Josh's brain, twisting him into knots. Reaching between them, Josh palmed his own cock and squeezed—hard. It should've crippled him. Instead, pre-cum leaked onto his stomach. He writhed beneath Dmitry, needing more. Dmitry shoved Josh's knee up and rammed his way inside without warning or preparation. The tearing of skin and burning flesh had an orgasm slamming into Josh without warning. Wave upon wave of pleasure rolled through Josh as Dmitry fucked him without mercy. Josh already knew there would be teeth marks covering his chest and claw marks running down his body after this. A second round of spasms hit Josh at the thought. He knew he was fucked in the head, but his anger and hurt needed an outlet. Not loving Dmitry wasn't an option for him, especially now that Josh knew the truth. He'd seen it in Dmitry's eyes. If there had been any other choice in the world for Dmitry, the man never would've taken Kon's life.

Chapter 6

"I need to head to the gym."

Dmitry looked up from his book and focused on Jozsua at the man's claim. For the most part, Jozsua hadn't left his sight since the night he'd shown up at Dmitry's door, looking for answers. Dmitry had been dreading the moment Jozsua got bored with being with him nonstop. Being as how Jozsua was now dressed to do exactly as he claimed, Dmitry surmised the moment had come. As much as Jozsua loved working out, he was surprised it had taken Jozsua this long, but he supposed he'd kept the man's body hard and busy in other ways. A smile pulled at his lips at the thought. He swallowed it down, refusing to let Jozsua see his pleasure and mistake it for him being fine with Jozsua leaving.

"Is this the same gym owned by your adolescent want-to-be lovers?"

Jozsua's lips twitched at Dmitry's question. He pressed them together, visibly fighting back a smile before answering. "That's where I pay a membership fee."

"No," Dmitry said, setting his book aside.

Jozsua failed to hide his smile this time. It exploded across his face. "That's it? Just no, huh?"

Dmitry didn't try sugarcoating things. If Jozsua liked Max and Ryan, he wouldn't be alone with them again. "We each speak three languages and all three are the same. No."

"So," Jozsua said, dragging out the word. "You want me to get fat and lose every match I enter? I'm not opposed to either. Just wondering."

Dmitry came to his feet. "Your looks matter not at all to me, but in this case, I've been hopeful and planned ahead." He waved for Jozsua to follow as he headed for the stairs. "It wasn't easy finding someone who could mount your bag properly, but all your equipment has stayed with me since you left." He glanced over his shoulder. "I told you I left nothing of ours behind." Dmitry led Jozsua up the stairs to the room he'd converted into a gym. The punching bag, everything Jozsua had used to train in Texas, Dmitry had kept.

Jozsua eyed the steel beam crossing the ceiling and holding the weight of his heavy bag. "Wow. You made sure it wouldn't fall."

"Of course," Dmitry said. "It will withstand your powerful hit." He winked as he said the words, because—goddamn. Jozsua was sexy and powerful and his. It was intoxicating.

"You know what else would go well with that steel beam," Jozsua said. His eyes flashed with mischief, fascinating Dmitry. "Chains. Kind of like the ones they have at Affinity."

Dmitry sucked in a deep breath, hoping to combat the wave of lust that overcame him at Jozsua's taunt. He ran his tongue over his teeth, trying to hold back the demons. Dmitry could hurt Jozsua. Get his attention. Keep it focused on him. "It's been a very long time since you truly submitted to me." Dmitry heard the growl in his voice. He couldn't stop it from happening. Even when chained, Jozsua was the one who held all the power in their relationship. He wondered what would happen if Jozsua ever realized it.

Jozsua's gaze flashed with hunger. "You haven't asked me to."

Dmitry tilted his chin up and stared at the ceiling, hoping to hide his longing. Fuck it. "I'll find a tape measure and we'll figure out how long these chains need to be." Jozsua's laughter followed Dmitry from the room. He didn't realize he was smiling until his face smoothed of all emotion at the sound of the doorbell. No one came here. Not ever. Moving quietly, Dmitry checked the peephole. He bit back a growl at the sight of Gio Conti on the other side. What the fuck was he doing here? The last thing Dmitry needed was a Vegas crime boss in his house, especially with Jozsua right upstairs, showing his one weakness in the world.

While doing his best to keep his emotions hidden, Dmitry answered the door. The man's dark hair was styled to perfection, but his suit was cheap and his smile was fake. Dmitry didn't feel anything at all. He could kill the man right then and get back to his husband.

"Gio. This is a surprise."

"I'm sure it is," Gio said, tempting fate with his rude answer. He glanced over his shoulder as if checking for prying eyes. "May I come in and chat for a minute, Mr. Salko?"

Dmitry took a step back, silently inviting him inside. He motioned Gio toward his office. There were at least three guns in there. Damn. Jozsua was upstairs. He needed to play nice. "What brings you by today?" Dmitry asked the moment Gio's ass hit one of Jozsua's nana's chairs.

"Rumor has it, you've been at Warehouse the past two weekends in a row. Understandably, that makes my people nervous," Gio said, coming straight to the point and easing Dmitry's annoyance a hair.

Naturally, the man would wonder over Dmitry's presence inside his fight club. People in Gio's business didn't see people in Dmitry's line of work unless business was bad for everyone.

A flash of blue caught Dmitry's eye before he could respond. Jozsua bounded down the stairs. Dmitry quickly moved to the doorway while trying not to draw attention to his actions. He met Jozsua's stare.

"Hey, did I hear the doorbell?"

Dmitry warned Jozsua with his gaze to be quiet before closing the door in his face.

"Was that Josh Salko?" Gio dragged out Jozsua's last name, as if all the clues he needed clicked together in his mind. "Sorry, Mr. Salko, I didn't realize Josh was a relation of yours. If I had, we could've been doing business."

Dmitry claimed the seat across from Gio. "He is my husband. No one does business with him but me." He knew he was talking double-speak, and he hoped Gio now thought Jozsua was in the same business as Dmitry.

A line appeared between Gio's dark eyes. "I thought you'd married Danshov's brother."

"Yes."

The line deepened. "There haven't been any rumors of the Danshovs setting up shop in Vegas since Konstantin's deportation. This is disturbing news."

Dmitry mentally calculated the distance to his gun. He'd hate to ruin the carpet in his office... and Nana's chair. "There are no Danshovs left on US soil. Jozsua is a Salko. There's no business here but ours." With each word Dmitry spoke, his face hardened a hair more. "If we're no longer welcome at Warehouse District, we'll accept your decision, of course. I recognize it's Conti territory."

Gio shifted in his seat and his gaze nervously shot around the room. "No, Mr. Salko, that wasn't my intention. Of course, you're welcome there. However..."

Fuck.

"... as much I'd like to believe you, we both know Boris Danshov ran the underground bouts in your country. I can't risk Danshovs moving into my area. We'd feel better if Josh would agree to fight under contract with us if he plans to enter any matches in the future. Underground Vegas is—as you said—Conti territory, after all."

Ice filled Dmitry's veins. His voice

showed it. "Jozsua belongs to me. He contracts with no one." As the words passed his lips, Dmitry caught sight of a lit green light on the intercom system. Jozsua was listening to every word. Dmitry's stomach churned.

Gio stood. "I just stopped by to make sure we're good. Now that I know you were only visiting Warehouse to watch your husband fight, I can reassure my family of their safety. I can reassure them, right?"

"Of course," Dmitry said, attempting to hang on to a cordial tone. "Otherwise, you never would've known I was there," Dmitry added, in case Gio thought to approach Jozsua with his offer. Gio shifted nervously at the truth and threat in Dmitry's words. "I'll show you out."

The light on the intercom flashed red. Dmitry motioned Gio toward the door. It was impressive the way Gio managed to find the door and keep one eye locked on Dmitry at all times. Dmitry didn't draw another easy breath until Gio was gone. The instant he let down his guard, the pain sank in. Loving Jozsua did nothing for the man except steal everything Jozsua cared about. First Konstantin and now Jozsua's fighting career. When he'd married Jozsua, he'd yearned to give the man the world. Instead, he'd stolen Jozsua's life—one brick at a time.

He found Jozsua in the living room, staring into space. Without a qualm, Dmitry went down onto his knees between Jozsua's. Jozsua's eyes seemed to snap back into focus as his gaze locked on Dmitry. A sad smile touched Jozsua's lips.

"You're so fucking sexy on your knees. It's even hotter because I know you'd never get down on them for anyone else."

Instead of responding, Dmitry brought

Jozsua's hand to his mouth and pressed a kiss to the center of Jozsua's palm. His eyes fell closed as the weight of his failures settled on his shoulders. "The day I asked you to marry me, I had all these plans to make your every dream come true. I just didn't realize it would be your every nightmare."

Something dark flashed in Jozsua's eyes. "Is that what you think?"

Dmitry didn't respond.

Jozsua sat forward and kept coming, leaving Dmitry no choice but to sprawl out onto the floor. Jozsua snagged the front of Dmitry's shirt, easing him down, and keeping him from getting hurt in the fall. Not that Dmitry cared about his well-being. The way Jozsua watched him as he covered Dmitry's body with his own kept Dmitry captivated.

"Before you, there was nothing," Jozsua said, losing none of his intensity. "Konstantin kept me so hidden from the world, some days I wondered if I really didn't exist. Fighting was all I had. Then you came along, and everything was different. Colors seemed brighter. Food tasted better. After you were gone, the world plunged back into a dull haze. Everything is less without you."

"I didn't want to stay away," Dmitry said, confessing something he should have before now. "You hated me, and every day I died a little more because of it. Now, because of me—"

Jozsua captured Dmitry's lips, cutting off his words. Between Jozsua's massive weight and all-consuming kiss, Dmitry could barely draw a breath. His head spun. He no longer knew if it was due to lack of oxygen or love. Dmitry didn't care.

He'd never feared death. Dying this way would be a beautiful thing. Jozsua's mouth moved to Dmitry's jaw and air came rushing back to him. He sucked in a deep breath as Jozsua's teeth scraped down the cords of his neck. Dmitry tilted his chin up, giving Jozsua better access to his throat. The man's biting kisses bordered on painful as he slid down Dmitry's body. Dmitry's dick had never been harder. With a twist and swipe, Jozsua ripped every button from Dmitry's shirt, tearing it open. The show of strength had Dmitry struggling to breathe once more.

Countless times Jozsua had tongued the tattoo of his name permanently inked on Dmitry's side. He did it again now. Jozsua's soft hair twisted between Dmitry's fingers as he tried holding on. A rumble of laughter vibrated against his skin as Jozsua easily slipped from his hold. Soft lips brushed his navel. Dmitry's back arched in response. The front of his pants opened. Jozsua's hand dove inside, freeing Dmitry's erection. His touch was gentle in comparison to his kiss. The memory of their first kiss drifted through Dmitry's mind again, just as it had a million times before. He'd been so surprised by how sweetly Jozsua kissed. His crazy-colored hair and rough and tumble ways had given Dmitry the expectation of coarse treatment. Instead, Jozsua was a worshipper. It was so goddamn hot, Dmitry always expected his skin to melt. Jozsua sucked dick the same way he kissed—soft and sweet. It always made Dmitry think his mind would snap. The gentle lapping of Jozsua tongue teased at pleasure. There was no recreating the sensation. Without Jozsua in his life, there had only been the gnawing memory of his touch, slowly eating at the last dregs of Dmitry's sanity.

He held his breath, waiting for Jozsua

to take him between his lips, giving him back those sensations he'd craved. Jozsua took his time, dragging out the anticipation. He'd forgotten that part too—the way Jozsua teased, toying with him for minutes, the man made it feel like hours. His nose touched Dmitry's crown. Dmitry's hips left the floor. His body pled for mercy. Jozsua moved lower, placing light kisses down Dmitry's length. Dmitry's dick leaked. A drop of pre-cum escaped. Jozsua captured it on his tongue. Dmitry watched it happen. He couldn't tear his gaze away from Jozsua's every move. The man's expression didn't match his touch. He looked hard, as if barely keeping his lust in check. The knowledge soothed some of Dmitry's impatience.

Jozsua dragged his tongue up Dmitry's length while holding his gaze. "Tell me what you want, Dmitry."

In spite of his breathless state, Dmitry

didn't hesitate. "I want your brand of per-secution."

A low-sounding chuckle vibrated against Dmitry's cock, making him pant. He kissed Dmitry's hip. "No. I don't think I will." Dmitry spread his arms wide in surrender while staring at the ceiling. A bark of laughter escaped him. Even to his ears it sounded crazy. Jozsua got him fucking high with his fearless behavior. His body screamed for release, but his mind was in hyper-drive. When he was alone, Dmitry felt nothing at all. With Jozsua around, Dmitry felt everything all at once. "Never mind," Jozsua said with laughter sounding heavy in his voice. "This is too good to pass up," Jozsua added before swallowing Dmitry's dick.

It was everything Dmitry remembered and more. The torturous gentle lapping of Jozsua's tongue. The light suction, barely teasing at full-blown pleasure. Just when he thought Jozsua had finally fallen into a pattern he could follow to explosion, Jozsua changed angles and lightened his touch, nearly causing Dmitry to scream and curse.

Jozsua pulled away and gently brushed his lips to Dmitry's crown. "Tell me you love me."

"I love you," Dmitry dutifully said, because it was true and Jozsua wanted it.

The man's tongue teased Dmitry's slit, making Dmitry whimper. "Tell me how you'll make me pay for this."

At Jozsua's demand, Dmitry ran down a list of sexual torture even he couldn't remember once it left his lips. When he reached a bit about hours of edging with little to no direct contact with Jozsua's cock, the man's throat finally squeezed Dmitry's dick and finger curled inside Dmitry's ass, pressing hard on his prostate. The pressure that had beating down

Dmitry's crown exploded into a blinding orgasm, filling Jozsua's mouth with hot cum. Jozsua didn't let up. He sucked every last wave of ecstasy from Dmitry and then kept going for good measure. If he took a single breath, Dmitry didn't remember doing so. All he could think about was the heat surrounding his cock. Jozsua had no idea how patient Dmitry could be. If he'd decided to shut Dmitry out of his life for fifty years, it would've changed nothing. Dmitry would've still been right here waiting for Jozsua to notice he hadn't gone anywhere. Jozsua could walk away and find someone else to love him, but he'd never find anyone who matched Dmitry's sick and twisted level of fixation. Love can fade. Crazy obsession is to the grave.

*

Having Dmitry spent and limp beneath

him was a power trip Josh couldn't describe. Josh was the only person who ever saw Dmitry in this state. It went beyond all description, knowing he could do anything to him in that moment, and Dmitry would let it happen. Because he needed Dmitry's bare skin against his own, Josh pulled Dmitry to his feet and stripped all remnants of clothing from his body before leading him down the hall to bed. He pulled back the covers and urged Dmitry onto his back. Josh slowly stripped while Dmitry stared at him with a heated gaze.

Josh knew it said crazy things about him that it made him twice as horny, knowing Dmitry had already gotten off. He climbed on top of the man he loved, letting his erection brush Dmitry's overheated skin as he went. A hiss left Dmitry's lips. Josh's dick leaked at the sound. Neither of them were right in the head. Crazed-sounding laughter escaped Josh at the thought. Dmitry eyed him as if he knew exactly what Josh was thinking.

"You're savoring the thought of coating my body in cum, aren't you?" Dmitry asked, proving Josh right.

"Oh, yeah," Josh said, breathing in the moment. "You belong to me, to do with as I please. Right now, I want you to watch me jacking off on your gorgeous body."

Dmitry linked his fingers behind his head and settled in for a show. "I've got nothing but time."

While straddling Dmitry's body, Josh dragged his crown down the man's sexy abs and line of hair leading to Dmitry's dick. The way Dmitry chewed his bottom lip while he watched Josh's every move was enough to fuck with any man's mind. As much as Josh wanted to observe Dmitry's every reaction, Josh needed to taste the man's lips even more. He was already on the edge from teasing Dmitry.

When their mouths clashed, Josh's pumped faster. The flavor of Dmitry's tongue coated Josh's taste buds combined with every place their bodies met and the knowledge of everything Dmitry could do to his mind had Josh exploding before he was ready. Sounds he couldn't control tore from his throat. Dmitry swallowed them. They were a mess, and it was beautiful.

Balling up the sheet, Josh tried swiping away most of the mess before rolling to his side and taking Dmitry with him. He held the man tight, refusing to let any space come between them. There'd been too many nights he'd craved this man to let anything stand in his way now that he had Dmitry back in his arms. He knew Dmitry was angry over the Conti situation. Oddly, Josh was not. He'd been fighting his whole life. At first, it had been because it was expected of him. Then he'd fought because his anger needed an outlet. Now, he was simply tired and wanted to hold his husband.

More than that, Josh wanted to soak up every second and hang on to all the things he'd been missing. Kon and Kip—they were right about everything. Dmitry was his other half. They would never be normal, so they needed to embrace what they had for the wonder it was. Even if Josh could ever find it in his heart to care for anyone else, he would always be missing this deep pit of infatuation he shared with Dmitry. No one else would ever fit either of them. So, no, he didn't care if he ever fought again.

"You realize this house is compromised," Josh said, opening a discussion they needed to have.

Dmitry's hold tightened. "I'll take care of everything. Don't think about it."

"I want to, because we need a safe place to call home."

The soft brush of Dmitry's fingers along Josh's ribs stopped. Slowly, Dmitry shifted onto his elbow and met Josh's stare. His face was devoid of all emotion. "Do you mean that?"

Instead of answering, Josh finished his thoughts. "There's this cabin, near the springs on our land, it's really nothing more than a small hunting cabin. We'd be under each other's feet all the time, and you'd definitely get sick of me, but no one would find us." When Dmitry didn't respond and only kept staring at him as if waiting for more, nervous chatter set in. "We could help Kip raise my niece or travel. Maybe, for a little while, we could do nothing at all but be together. I guess it sounds mundane to you," Josh said when Dmitry's expression still didn't change.

"Is that really the life you want? Living in hiding? Pretending to be someone else?"

In spite of the heavy topic, Josh smiled. "I won't be pretending. No matter where we are, I'm always the same person—your husband. As long as I'm that, I'm not hiding or running. I'm exactly where I'm supposed to be. Home."

*

Home. Dmitry was speechless. In his head, he had a thousand things to say. He loved this man. Jozsua would never want for anything else so long as Dmitry lived. They would do everything Jozsua wanted whenever the man wanted for the rest of their lives. Raise Jade. Travel. What the fuck ever as long they were together, Dmitry didn't care. There were so many thoughts in his head, they crowded in Dmitry's throat and nothing happened. He kept staring at Jozsua, incapable of speech.

His cell phone rang, startling him from his thoughts. Since there were only a handful of people who knew how to reach him, and it only happened in times of emergency, Dmitry shot from the bed and went in search of the device. It was on the bedroom floor. He honestly had no clue how it had ended up there. Kipley's name showed on the face and Dmitry quickly pressed the phone to his ear.

"What's happened?"

"This man called, and he said something about Jade and Josh, and he knew who we were. Oh my fucking God, Dmitry. I didn't know who else to call. I pulled Jade out of school and came straight home, but now I'm afraid to ever take her back or leave the house. He knew us."

Every muscle in Dmitry's body hardened, poising for attack. "Take a breath." Dmitry waited until Kip did as he demanded. "Now, start over."

When Kip spoke again, it was slower. "I got a call from a guy named Gio. He said

214

he wanted me to pass a message on to Josh."

At Gio's name, Dmitry went from being the person who he was with Jozsua to work mode. "And this message?"

"He said Josh needs to come to Warehouse to discuss some things, and not to keep them waiting too long. Then he added, by the way, he has a beautiful niece." Rage froze Dmitry's blood, but Kip was crying now and he needed her calm. "He's talking about my daughter, Dmitry. My baby. The only piece of Kon I have left. My whole fucking world."

"And you said you are home now?" Dmitry asked, holding his calm in the face of her panic.

Kip took a breath as if attempting to control her hysteria. "Yes. I'm not sure I'll ever let her out of my sight again."

"I'll take care of it. Given the circumstances, you shouldn't leave the house

215

again today. I'm sending Jozsua to you. By tomorrow, everything will be back to normal."

At his name, Jozsua sat up. "What's going on?"

Dmitry held his hand up, silently asking the man to wait. "Kipley, I promised Konstantin. You know I won't let anything happen to any of you."

Her voice still shook, but she seemed calmer. "I know. I trust you."

That was why he would never let her down. "Jozsua is on his way."

"Okay."

With his reassurance in place, Dmitry disconnected the call and focused on Jozsua. "I need you to go to Kipley." Jozsua leapt from the bed, looking more than a little worried, and sexy as hell in his nudity. "Gio has made a veiled threat in regard to Jade if you don't come to Warehouse to discuss a contract."

"What?" Jozsua's furious roar was every bit as hot as his body. "I'll snap that little fucker's neck."

Dmitry pulled some clothes on, calculating his every move while Jozsua continued his rant.

"How fucking dare he drag Kip and Jade into anything, especially since he knows she's a Danshov. Oh my God," Jozsua breathed. "Unless he's spoken with someone from the Danshov family and they've come up with some kind of way to trap us all again."

"No," Dmitry said, putting an end to Jozsua's growing fears. "I have... reassurances in place. If he'd contacted anyone, I would know. No," Dmitry repeated. "This is him alone, and showing a serious lack of care for breathing. Now, please, go to Kipley. She is upset and needs your strength."

Jozsua's entire demeanor shifted. His

217

expression went blank in a valid attempt at hiding his emotions, but his eyes gave him away. They were filled with pain. "Don't do this to me twice. The last time you sent me to Kip, you didn't come back. Maybe I should just make a deal with Gio?"

Dmitry needed to hurry, but Jozsua needed reassurance. Jozsua won. After closing the distance between them, Dmitry cupped Jozsua's face, giving him no other choice but to hold Dmitry's stare. "No. Whoever controls you controls me, and that'll never happen. I will always come back to you. This cabin you spoke of, meet me there at ten tonight. I swear to you I will be there. But right now, I need you to go to Kip. It's imperative you go now, in case Gio grows bold."

Dmitry's warning sank in and got Jozsua moving. The way his man openly accepted Dmitry's word had Dmitry recalculating his plan. He would have to be faster than usual if he hoped to make the ten o'clock deadline.

Chapter 7

Josh expected to find a freaked out Kip when he arrived home. Instead, she was calm—eerily so. If Jade felt anything off inside their home, she didn't show it. She was her usual high-energy self. It ended up being him who couldn't withstand the waiting. By nine, Kip put him out of the house.

"Cam will be home in a few minutes. You should go."

Josh snorted and twisted at his fingers, trying to hide his rising panic. "Are you kicking me out of my own house?"

Kip held his gaze and Josh realized something he should've noticed already. Her calm was a façade. Inside, she was freaking the fuck out. "When Cam gets home, you don't need to be here. If he doesn't see you, he can't disprove you weren't where you claimed to be. You know, when and if Dmitry needs an alibi."

After closing the distance between them, Josh pressed a quick kiss to Kip's forehead. "If anything happens, I'll be right outside, lurking out of sight."

For a moment, Kip clung to him. "Dmitry won't let anything happen to us."

Jesus, his brother had been so lucky to have Kip. "I know."

With a final shove, she had him moving for the door. "Now go before Cam sees you."

Josh rambled around outside, trying to pass the time. Every time he checked his phone for the time, it was a minute later than the last. His nerves couldn't take it. The theory of relativity was kicking his ass. If Dmitry had been there with him, staring at the beautiful springs and enjoying the night sky, time would have flown. Now that he was waiting, praying for everything to be okay, time screeched to a halt before crawling away like a snail.

At ten till ten, Josh couldn't stand any more. He picked his way through the trees and headed for the building hidden nearby. If he was early, then he'd wait. Anything had to be better than this constant staring at the face of his phone, praying for the numbers to change. The tiny wooden structure came into view. Josh bit back a growl at the sight.

The cabin was dark. There wasn't a car in the driveway and—as far as Josh could tell—no movement inside. His heart fell at the sight. He'd wanted to trust Dmitry. Wanted it with every fiber of his being. Every step he took toward the cabin felt like another nail in the coffin of his life. Being with Dmitry again had sent him back to that place where he hoped for more. If life had taught him anything, it was that hope was a fool's game. Still, he headed for the door, praying Dmitry was only running late. He could show up at any moment. Lying to himself was Josh's favorite pastime.

The black mood coating his brain dissipated when the doorknob turned beneath his hand without unlocking it. When the smell of burning candles reached his nose, his happiness notched up even higher. Dmitry was here. The flicker of candlelight spilled from the kitchen and danced on the walls of the living room. Josh's feet carried him toward the flames, like he was the moth.

Josh found Dmitry lighting candles on the kitchen table. He glanced up as Josh entered the room. With the tiny lights dancing on Dmitry's cheekbones, the man looked like a ghost. Sometimes, Josh felt like Dmitry wasn't real. Without a doubt, Josh knew Dmitry could disappear without a trace at any moment.

Dmitry blew out the long match he'd

been using. "You're early. I wanted to surprise you."

Josh took in the food sitting on the table and the mood lighting. This man would be the death of him. While Josh had been panicking, Dmitry had been preparing. "I couldn't wait any longer. When I saw the place was still dark and no car in the drive, I got worried."

After moving to one end of the table, Dmitry pulled out a chair and motioned for Josh to sit. "I no longer have a car. It went up in flames, along with the house."

The temptation to ask for details—like how in the hell Dmitry had gotten there—was overwhelming but didn't matter. Dmitry was there. Life was complete. He moved across the room. Before reaching the chair, Josh snagged Dmitry around the waist, determined to taste the man's lips and kill the last remnants of terror still scratching at his spine. A hiss of pain escaped Dmitry, reverberating off the walls of the kitchen. Josh released Dmitry and took a step back. A dark stain appeared on Dmitry's light-colored shirt. For a moment, all Josh could do was watch it grow while his mind came to terms with what his eyes showed him. Dmitry was hurt. Once the realization hit, Josh ripped open the man's shirt.

"What the fuck happened?" There was a nasty-looking gash in Dmitry's side. It had been stitched but was still seeping. "Oh my God. Did you stitch this yourself?"

"Someone had to do it," Dmitry answered, sounding weak.

Josh's gaze shot to the man's face. He looked, really looked at Dmitry, and realized the real reason he'd thought Dmitry looked like a ghost in the candlelight. His face was pale, making the dark circles beneath his eyes stand out.

"Jesus fucking Christ, Dmitry. What

are you doing serving dinner like nothing happened?" As he asked the question, Josh forced Dmitry to accept his help and headed for the hall. Anger became full-blown panic when Dmitry leaned most of his weight into Josh, as if he wouldn't make it under his own power.

"You mean more than I do," Dmitry said, as if that answered everything. "I knew you would sit around worrying and skip dinner."

Josh ground his teeth, attempting to hold the flood of emotion racing through him at bay. He lost the battle. "Tell me right fucking now, Dmitry Salko, what I'm up against. What happened? Can I expect company any second?"

"Gio is a knife man, apparently, which is something I would've known if I'd had time to study his habits. You have nothing to fear, baby. There isn't a Conti left to come calling." No Contis left. *Holy shit.*

Dmitry's steps slowed even further and his weight increased. Josh picked up the speed, sweeping Dmitry into the first bed they came to. "No doubt there will be some other family who will step up and take their place with the underground, but no one who knows about you."

"Seriously, Dmitry. You think I give a fuck about my fighting career?"

Dmitry's eyes were closed, as if barely hanging on to consciousness. "The night you told me you had to give up your run for the championship, you looked so sad. I've never forgotten it." Dmitry's voice weakened by the moment. "I wanted to steal you away right then and make life different for you. Done nothing but fail you," Dmitry said as he passed out.

Josh stared at Dmitry's still form until his eyes burned from not blinking. He needed to see his husband's chest moving up and down in time with his breathing like Josh needed oxygen to survive. Once he was certain Dmitry was truly only unconscious, he rushed through the cabin, finding everything he needed to clean Dmitry's wound. Josh thanked the stars Dmitry didn't stir through the entire ordeal. The peroxide he poured on the man's skin bubbled for way longer than Josh cared to see. He didn't stop until the fluids ran clean. Next came the scolding hot water and clean bandages. Dmitry hadn't done a bad job of stitching himself up, all things considered.

He did his best to keep Dmitry clean and comfortable. Josh lost all concept of time as he sat at Dmitry's side. When the man stirred, fighting an invisible foe, Josh climbed in beside him and held on. The moment their skin met, Dmitry sucked in a deep breath. It sounded so much like a happy sigh that Josh found himself smiling in spite of everything. Dmitry would be fine. He couldn't let himself think otherwise. When Josh had lost Konstantin, his grief had run deep. Those days would be nothing in comparison if anything ever happened to Dmitry. It had been one thing to know the man was alive somewhere in the world, even if they weren't together. He couldn't imagine any scenario where Dmitry wasn't there anymore at all.

"Nana's chairs went up in the blaze," Dmitry's said, startling Josh. He hadn't known the man was truly awake. He searched Dmitry's face. His eyes were still closed and Josh still wasn't convinced Dmitry wasn't talking in his sleep. Still, he answered, hoping to soothe Dmitry just in case.

"It's okay."

"But what about your childhood memories," Dmitry argued, sounding lucid.

Happiness burst to life in Josh's chest. A chuckle escaped him in his relief. Dmitry would be okay. "They're just chairs, Dmitry. In the grand scheme of things, they matter not at all."

"But your nana sang to you in those chairs."

Josh swallowed back a snort. "She also turned me over her knee many times in those chairs, so no, they're no loss."

A line appeared between Dmitry's closed eyes. "The bed and piano are gone too."

"I'll buy us new ones," Josh said, hoping Dmitry calmed down soon. He didn't need the man getting upset over trivial shit.

"Okay." As Dmitry agreed, his muscles relaxed. Josh bit back a sigh of relief. Dmitry stiffened again in Josh's arms. His eyes shot open. "Jozsua."

The panic in Dmitry's tone had Josh on edge. "Yeah?"

"I wanted to be normal for you. I should've told you that every day."

Josh's eyes burned with unshed tears. He tightened his hold on Dmitry while trying not to hurt him. "That's funny, because I never—not for one second—wanted you to be anything or anyone other than who and what you are."

Dmitry's breathing deepened, letting Josh know he'd drifted back to sleep. In spite of the fear sitting on Josh's throat, his eyelids grew heavy while listening to the steady beat of Dmitry's heart. His muscles relaxed. They wouldn't be apart again. Even if Dmitry slipped away from this life, Josh would choose to go with him.

* * *

A loud banging pulled Josh from his sleep. He rushed for the door before the sound woke up Dmitry. When he swung the door wide, Kip burst inside with Jade on her hip. "What happened?" Kip asked, letting Jade slide to floor. The little girl was off before Kip had time to pull Josh in for a hug. "I've been trying to call, but your cell-phone goes straight to voicemail. Cameron got a call on his radio, saying the Conti family was killed when a gas line exploded during a family get together at a friend's house. They were saying the family friend was dead too, and I hadn't heard from you, and damn it Josh, I was freaking the fuck out." Kip punctuated her claim by punch-ing Josh in the arm. He was still trying to absorb every word she said while blinking off sleep. "Cameron was just like—not my jurisdiction, and all I could think was—I know that address. It was Dmitry's house."

"How do you know where Dmitry lives?"

"Don't you worry about that," Kip fussed. "I was scared shitless something had happened to Dmitry."

Josh shook his head. "He's okay," Josh lied. For some reason he couldn't explain, he couldn't force his lips to shape the words, letting Kip know the man he loved more than life had been stabbed. He motioned toward the bedroom. "He's sleeping."

Kip's gaze moved in the direction Josh pointed before returning to hold his stare. "A buddy of Cameron's says there's zero evidence the explosion was anything other than a tragic accident. So, there's that."

Thankfully, Kip just looked relieved for everything to be over, because Josh was barely holding his shit together. Dmitry had been stabbed. He could've died. It was just another day in his life, but it was days he'd thought he'd left behind.

Kip cast a glance around the room. "Where did Jade go?"

They both turned toward the bedroom. He'd left the door standing open. Jade's chipper voice filled the air, talking faster than any man could keep up with. As one, they headed for the open doorway. When Jade and Dmitry came into view, Josh bit back a laugh in spite of his internal freak out. He couldn't lose this man. Dmitry and Jade sat face to face on the bed while Jade showed off a bruise on her knee. She spoke a mile a minute, but Dmitry kept nodding along, as if he understood every word.

"Tree, kiss it," Jade demanded.

Dmitry dutifully pressed a kiss to Jade's bruise. Jade's smile turned luminous as she threw her arms around Dmitry's neck and tried to climb his shoulders. Dmitry tried to hide a wince. Josh caught sight of his pained expression before it disappeared behind a mask. Josh rushed across the room. He snagged Jade and tossed her into the air before catching her again. Her loud squeal rent the air.

"What are you doing in here bugging Dmitry?" Kip asked, making a valid attempt at sounding stern.

"Tree pretty," Jade said, holding her arms out for Kip. Josh stopped himself from vehemently agreeing. Seeing Dmitry's beautiful eyes open and lucid was fucking beautiful.

Kip sighed as she took Jade from Josh's arms. "Jesus, I'm in so much trouble." She smoothed her hand over Jade's blonde curls. "Tree isn't your jungle gym and although he's very pretty, he's also looking kind of ragged, so let him get some sleep, okay?" Jade's bottom lip made an appearance, but Kip was having none of it. "*Anh*, don't start that. We'll come back later." Without waiting for Jade's agreement, Kip focused on Dmitry. Her eyes welled with tears, taking Josh by surprise. "Thank you," she mouthed before turning on her heel and leaving them alone. Josh watched her go, barely stopping his mouth from falling open. Only moments earlier, Kip had looked so put together. Now, she was showing cracks. Sometimes he forgot how good she was at pretending none of it got to her.

Unfortunately, Kip's gratitude didn't soothe Josh's fear. The moment they were alone, Josh met Dmitry's tired-looking gaze. For a moment, he simply stared at the man he loved more than life and took in his gorgeous face. "Tree is very pretty," Josh said to hide the delayed panic setting in.

Dmitry snorted. "Tree needs to pee."

Josh snorted but helped Dmitry to the bathroom. "Say that five times fast," Josh said before Dmitry closed the door in his face. It was a ridiculous attempt at stopping the words building in his throat. Josh sat on the bed and listened to Dmitry moving around inside the bathroom. The water ran and Josh focused on the sound, trying to force his mind to go blank. He couldn't do this. He couldn't not do this. The bathroom door opened and Josh shot to his feet. Dmitry looked steady, but pale.

He'd taken off his shirt. Josh's gaze moved over the man's body, soaking in every detail. They couldn't keep this up. There would be another mafia family. Another contract. Maybe one day Dmitry would get caught and go to prison or the next knife wouldn't miss. With every building thought came another brick on Josh's chest, piling on top of the one he still had from losing Kon. Dmitry stood still—waiting. He knew. The dam burst.

"I lied," Josh said, like ripping off a bandage. "Kon said I'd never have it, but I do want normal."

To Josh's surprise, Dmitry smiled and slowly crossed the room. When he reached Josh's side, he pushed until Josh was flat on his back and staring at the ceiling. He tried sitting up when Dmitry straddled his hips, pinning him to the bed.

"No. You'll tear open your stitches."

"Shut it," Dmitry fussed, making Josh fall silent. His expression turned serious as he stared down at Josh as if trying to decide where he should start. "Last night, that was about protecting what's mine. That's something I'll always do."

"I wouldn't expect anything less. Kip and Jade are family."

"And I believe I told you to hush," Dmitry said, making it obvious he wasn't feeling up to interruptions. "However, in spite of my falling off the wagon last night, I've been retired for two years now." Dmitry shook his head. "In fact, I've been downright boring, if you don't count stalking you. Hell, I bought a house in the suburbs for you. If that doesn't scream ordinary, I don't know what does."

Josh licked his lips, unsure he should interrupt yet. He couldn't take it. "Two years? What have you been doing with

239

yourself?"

Dmitry swayed. Josh's heart lurched until Dmitry's swapped positions, coming to rest on Josh's chest. Their bare skin pressed against each other. Dmitry released a happy-sounding sigh. "Much better," he said, sounding content. "I told you, I've been stalking you. This is what I've been holding out for, though—your skin against mine. Of course, in my fantasies, there were less stitches."

"Huh," Josh said for lack of anything more. "I expected it to be harder."

"Well, I did lose a lot of blood."

A snort escaped Josh at Dmitry's asinine comment. "I meant I expected you to argue or something."

Dmitry snuggled in as close as possible, as if seeking warmth. Josh snagged the comforter and covered them up.

"Thank you." The exhaustion in Dmitry's voice had Josh's heart turning over in his chest. "It's so cold in here. Nothing matters as much as you do, Jozsua. You're my Everglades snowflake. I want to stay like we are now. My whole life, I've been off in the head. You're the first healthy obsession I've ever had. If you want normal, that's what you'll get. We'll be the most unexceptional people for miles around."

Josh couldn't stop smiling. His cheeks ached from it. Dmitry spoke as if it would be so easy—simple. "Let's not get carried away," Josh argued, letting happiness carry away with his mouth. "I'm too kinky to fall too far down the boring well."

Dmitry held his stare. Light blue eyes so light in coloration they were definitely gray watched Josh with interest. Their heat had always been ten times hotter than anyone else's on the planet when he looked at Josh. It was an addiction Josh didn't care to shake. "I hope you never ask me to give up punishing you for loving me. We have a cabin in the woods now. No one can hear you scream or moan."

"I'd kill us both before letting you go."

A smile exploded across Dmitry's face at the threat. "The streets will run red before I ever let you get away."

"We're fucked in the head," Josh said, hearing his happiness in every word.

He felt more than saw Dmitry shrug. "What's it matter? We keep all the crazy locked up between us."

"Speaking of locked up," Josh said, hearing the sex dripping from every word. "Whatever happened to those handcuffs we used to have?"

"Went up in the blaze."

Josh settled deeper into the mattress, ready to hang on to Dmitry for life. "Probably for the best. You need to recover."

Dmitry's hand found its way between Josh's legs. He swiped Josh's growing erection before slipping Josh's zipper down. "I'm hurt. Not dead. You'd be amazed what I can still do at half capacity."

The tightening of his groin had Josh's voice turning husky. "You've kept me amazed since the first time we met, but I'm willing to let you try to impress me."

The evil-sounding laugh leaving Dmitry's lips almost had Josh ready to take back his taunt. He already knew Dmitry could be downright sadistic. Since Josh liked it, he held his silence and breath, waiting for Dmitry's next move. He was willing to bet good money—whatever it was—it would be completely insane and would steal Josh's breath. He couldn't fucking wait.

The End

Author Bio

Charity Parkerson is an award winning and multi-published author with several companies. Born with no filter from her brain to her mouth, she decided to take this odd quirk and insert it in her characters.

*2015 Readers' Favorite Award Winner
*Winner of 2, 2014 Readers' Favorite Awards
*2015 Passionate Plume Award Finalist
*2013 Readers' Favorite Award Winner
*2013 Reviewers' Choice Award Winner
*2012 ARRA Finalist for Favorite Paranormal Romance
*Five-time winner of The Mistress of the Darkpath

Connect with her online:

--Website: charityparkerson.com
--Facebook: facebook.com/authorCharityParkerson
facebook.com/TheMenofSin
--Twitter: twitter.com/CharityParkerso